THE
SUMMER
PEOPLE

Books by John Rowe Townsend

THE SUMMER PEOPLE

GOOD NIGHT, PROF, DEAR

THE INTRUDER

TROUBLE IN THE JUNGLE
(originally *Gumble's Yard*)

PIRATE'S ISLAND

GOOD-BYE TO THE JUNGLE

THE SUMMER PEOPLE

by JOHN ROWE TOWNSEND

J. B. LIPPINCOTT COMPANY

Philadelphia and New York

U.S. Library of Congress Cataloging in Publication Data

Townsend, John Rowe.
  The summer people.

  SUMMARY: In the summer of 1939 a sixteen-year-old boy and girl
considered the "perfect couple" by their families secretly begin seeing
and falling in love with another girl and boy.
  [1. England—Fiction] I. Title.
PZ7.T6637Su3   [Fic]   72-3270
ISBN-0-397-31421-3

THE SUMMER PEOPLE

From Eastpool →

North Bay

Eastpool Road

Holiday bungalows

Bay Road

Railway Station →

Top Square

The Beck

SMUGGLERS' COVE
formerly
Linley Bottom

A.M. JAUSS

Cliff path

Imperial Hotel

Middle Row

Main Street

Bottom Square

The slipway

To Craven Head →

South Bay

The Rocks

Smugglers' Cove,
England,
23rd September, 1972

Dear Stephen and Carolyn,
   You'll be surprised at receiving this bulky airmail package of typescript. When I got your joint letter a few weeks ago, I hoped at first to see you before the great day. But that is not going to happen. You have no plans to visit England, and I feel that it would embarrass us all if I flew out to the West Coast of America to tell you this long story in person. So I have put it all on paper. I admit I didn't think when I began that the pile of typewritten sheets would be quite so thick.
   I could hardly blame you if you put it aside un-read. So let me tell you by way of introduction that this narrative is about a group of young people, and

about two young people in particular. One is myself, when I was not quite seventeen. The other is a girl called Ann Tarrant.

I know that name will startle you, and I'm sorry. But I think it will make you want to read what I have written. Perhaps I'd better assure you at once that there's nothing in this account which could cause you to change your plans.

I've described many incidents and conversations as if I could remember them exactly. Of course I can't—not after a third of a century. But basically this narrative is accurate. And by the time you've read it you will know why I felt the story had to be told.

Sincerely,

Philip Martin

1

Nowadays they call the village Smugglers' Cove, but that's just to attract tourists. For centuries it was Linley Bottom. After the last war the local council decided they had to do something about a name like that, and Smugglers' Cove was the result.

The smugglers were genuine enough, but they died out more than 150 years ago. Then, for over a century, Linley Bottom was just a poor fishing village. It was and is a maze of little old houses, joined on to each other at odd angles and different levels, and linked by winding, cobbled alleyways. The alleys lead from one to another until they come to the main street, which straggles down from Top Square to the tiny beach they still call the Bottom. Here you may still see a few boats drawn up, perhaps a few nets and a few lobster pots.

By the nineteen-thirties the summer people were moving into Linley Bottom. Some of them bought old cottages in the village and smartened them up. If they were wise they avoided buying houses too near the east cliff, for the sea gnaws steadily at Linley, and every year a little of it crumbles away.

Others among the summer people built holiday bungalows at North Bay, a mile or so from the Bottom. This was not too convenient for the village, but close to a good beach, and untouched by coast erosion. My own family and their friends the Pillings and Foxes all owned bungalows. Ours was called The Anchor; the Pillings', though only a modest pink brick structure like the rest, was Cliff Lodge, and the Foxes' was Shangri-La.

Apart from summer residents, most of Linley's visitors stayed at the Imperial Hotel, on a ridge halfway between the Bottom and North Bay. There were no hotels or guest-houses in the village itself, and very few trippers came for the day. Linley didn't seem as picturesque then as it does now, and the road along the coast was narrow and full of potholes. The only other link with civilization was the little steam train that chuffed its way around the bay half a dozen times a day from Eastpool.

Come with me now to Linley Bottom in 1939. Meet our three families—the five Martins, the four Foxes, the three Pillings—as they arrive on a summer evening to begin their main holiday of the year. I can give you the date and time exactly. It is half past nine on Wednesday the second of August. We have driven in a little convoy of three cars from the city where we all live: out along the Roman road to the coast, then through the big resort of Eastpool, with its promenade and pier and pleasure beach and marine pavilion. At Eastpool we have bought a great pile of fish and chips, which we keep warm in thick wrappings of newspaper for the last ten miles along the winding road to Linley. Now we are about to eat it, in the Foxes' bungalow. This is, though we do not know it, the last time we shall ever arrive together for a holiday at Linley Bottom.

I am Philip Martin: sixteen years, ten months, and thirty days old. Because there are not enough seats to go round, I am sitting side by side on the same chair with Sylvia Pilling. Sylvia is also sixteen years, ten months, and thirty days old. She and I, although not related, are "twins"; we happen to have been born on the same day. Sylvia's father, who died three years ago, was my father's business partner.

Tonight, Sylvia and I are being teased. It begins when paunchy Mr. Fox brings out drinks to go with the meal: beer for the men, cider for the women, lemonade for the children. This year, for the first time, he pours beer for me and cider for Sylvia, accompanying it with facetious remarks about growing up, and warnings not to drink too much.

For years Sylvia and I have just been two of the youngsters. But with Mr. Fox's prompting everyone suddenly seems to notice that we are a young man and woman. I have grown taller since last year, and Sylvia more feminine.

"They make a handsome couple, don't they?" says Mrs. Pilling, looking at us fondly.

Actually I think my own appearance is rather ordinary; but Sylvia's is not. She has had far more than her share of nature's gifts. She is oval-faced, blue-eyed, clear-complexioned, with shining fair hair. She is also intelligent, good at games, and nice.

"I never realized," Mr. Fox tells Mrs. Pilling in tones of blunt admiration, "what a bonny lass your Sylvia is getting to be." And hints are dropped on all sides about a romantic attachment between us.

In fact there is no such thing. Sylvia and I have been

friends ever since we can remember. We tend to take each other for granted and look elsewhere for the romantic attachments. But the hints are embarrassing, all the same. Mr. Fox, who never knows when to stop, draws our attention to each other's attractions in rather frank terms, until quelled by a look from his wife. My elder sister Paula claims, maliciously, that Sylvia and I are blushing.

My mother puts a stop to it all by asking me to wash the dishes. This is a mild, familiar witticism; there are no dishes to wash. Crumpling the pile of newspaper that has held the fish and chips into a large untidy ball, I notice headlines to the effect that Germany is increasing its war preparations and that air-raid shelters are about to go on sale in England.

Now Rodney Fox comes to life. Rodney, who is dark, thin-faced, and eighteen, has pointedly ignored the previous conversation. But he sees these headlines and reads a couple of them aloud. Nobody makes any comment. Probably no one wants to think about such unpleasant matters when we are just beginning our summer holiday. But Rodney is insistent, and finishes up with the remark, "There's going to be a war, you know."

"That fellow Hitler?" says Mr. Fox. "Don't you believe it. It's only a matter of time till somebody calls his bluff. Then he'll back down. You'll see."

"I wouldn't count on it," says Rodney.

Mr. Fox ignores him and goes on, "As for Mussolini, I reckon he's just a laugh. When it comes to fighting, Eyeties are no bloody good, and Musso knows it."

This remark at least produces a response from other adults: not to what is said but to the words it is expressed in. "Bloody" is still strong language in England in 1939.

"Bernard!" says Mrs. Pilling, surprised.

"Bernie, please!" protests Mrs. Fox, who spends a good

deal of her life trying to damp down what she regards as the excesses of her husband, son, and daughter. "Don't let's have your public-bar expressions here. And in front of the children, too!"

Mr. Fox merely winks at us and says he expects we've heard ruder words than that. Now it is Mrs. Fox whose face reddens with embarrassment. And again my mother comes to the rescue, remarking that my small sister Alison is practically asleep and should be in bed, and that we all have our unpacking to do. In the general stir, the topic of impending war is lost.

But Rodney Fox's remarks have reminded me unpleasantly of discussions in our current affairs class at school. We have been talking about the actions of Adolf Hitler all term. Like other members of the class, I am all too well aware that I shall be of military age before long.

"I hope Rodney's wrong," I say to Sylvia as we walk away from the Foxes' door, "but I have an awful feeling he's probably right."

"So have I."

"I wonder if Hitler will let us have our five weeks' holiday before the balloon goes up."

"Or even let us get through to our birthday in peace," says Sylvia.

She and I often relate coming events to our joint birthday. A birthday is an unusual and pleasant thing to have in common, and we quite enjoy referring to ours. But this time, though we don't know it, the reference is altogether too apt. Our seventeenth birthday will be on the third of September, 1939—the first day of the Hitler war.

2

"I want to go to the beach," says my sister Alison, aged seven.

It's Thursday morning, our first morning in Linley. I am waiting for my father to appear. There is something I intend to tackle him about. So far, only my mother and Alison are up.

"I want to go to the beach," says Alison again.

"After breakfast," Mother tells her.

"I want to go now. I'll come back for breakfast."

Alison is a strong-willed, self-assertive little character, accustomed to holding her own as the youngest member by ten years of a family of five. Paula and I sometimes refer to her as the Afterthought.

"Nobody," says my mother, "but *nobody*, is going to the beach before breakfast. It'll be ready in a few minutes anyway. Go and tell Daddy and Paula to get dressed. . . . Oh, here's Daddy now. Anyway, Alison, go and hurry Paula up."

"Father," I say.

"Mmmm?"

"About that boat."

"What boat?"

"The sailing dinghy you promised to get."

"I didn't promise to get a sailing dinghy."

"Well, then, the sailing dinghy that I *thought* you promised to get."

"What about it?"

"We could still get one. You know the man who has the boatyard at Eastpool. He buys and sells them. We could go along and see what he has."

"Philip," my father says, "I'm sorry, but we can't afford to buy a sailing dinghy this year."

"But a few months ago you were talking as if we would."

"I only said we might. As a matter of fact, Phil, we've just had the latest figures from the accountant, and the business isn't making money. If it wasn't for the Army contract, we'd have to close down. It's as bad as that."

The business is a small clothing factory in our city. This year it has turned to making uniforms for the militiamen—the first intake of twenty-year-old conscripts.

"Anyway," my father goes on, "you need more experience before you own a boat. And I'm getting too old for sailing."

This last remark irritates me. My father is forty-six, a vigorous man who has always played outdoor games.

"I notice you've brought your golf clubs," I say sourly.

"Yes. Well . . ." For a moment Father seems shame-faced. "Bernie Fox and I have joined the Eastpool Golf Club as holiday members. It doesn't cost much, Phil, and we need the exercise. I could make you a member if you like. You could have a lesson or two from the professional."

"No, thank you. I don't want to play golf."

Then, surprising myself, I break out bitterly, "That's what it *really* is, isn't it? You're getting so keen on golf, you can't be bothered with what anybody else wants. You'll go off with old fatty Fox every day, refugees from family life, and we won't even see you."

Father says nothing. I know he is hurt. I know that he knows there's a sting of truth in what I've said. And as soon as I've said it I'm sorry, because really we get on well together as a rule. But I'm deeply frustrated about that boat. And—still to my own surprise—I find that I haven't finished.

"As for the business," I go on, "what you need is a nice war with *millions* of people called up, then you'll be all right."

There was a time when my father would not have taken that from me. But the time has passed. He turns on his heel and walks away quietly towards the back door.

"Philip!" my mother exclaims. "Oh, Phil, how *could* you? All that because you can't have a boat!"

"It's not just that."

"What your father said was absolutely true. There isn't money for a boat. If things don't get better we may have to sell this bungalow. And a month's membership of the golf club costs practically nothing. And I don't mind if he plays golf most days. It's good for him; he needs to relax."

"Well, if *you* don't mind. . . ." I say ungraciously. "After all, you have to cope with Alison while other people are away doing things."

"I have to cope with all four of you," Mother says. "and some of you take some coping with." She is quite calm. "Such as you, Phil. One day you're all grown up and the next you're . . ."

"Childish?"

"Well, you said it. Now go and apologize to your father. Especially for what you said about having a war. You know he wouldn't want a war just to save the business. . . . You've got war on your mind, haven't you, Phil?"

"Yes."

I go outside. Father is doing something to the car.

"I'm sorry," I say.

"That's all right, Phil." Very quietly. I wait, but the conversation seems to be over. I go indoors again. My sister Paula is just arriving from her bedroom, hand in hand with Alison.

"Did I hear sounds of domestic drama?" Paula inquires. "What was it all about?"

"Nothing, dear, nothing," Mother says calmly.

"I want to go to the beach," says Alison.

"*After* breakfast, Alison. It's ready now. Go and fetch Daddy."

Paula, Alison, and I sit down to eat. The girls are facing me. Over their shoulders I can see through an open door into the kitchen. Father has come in from outside. Mother embraces him. They stay like that, holding each other, for a minute or more. She is his strength, and he knows it.

The beach party is ready to move off. Nine people, laden with things to be carried down the path to the shore. Our families all share a beach chalet, but we don't leave anything in it when we're not at Linley. So there are deckchairs, canvas windbreaks, cooking utensils, water-carriers, a picnic basket, bats and balls and wickets: all kinds of things to be taken down at the start of the holiday.

Nine people. My father, Paula and I; Mrs. Pilling and Brian; Mr. and Mrs. Fox, Rodney and Brenda. Altogether there are twelve of us in the three families, but three are missing. My mother, yielding to Alison's demands, has taken her down to the beach already. Sylvia Pilling is unaccounted for.

"Where is she? Where's Philip's sweetheart?" demands Mr. Fox, who is marshalling the expedition.

"Really, Bernard!" Mrs. Pilling protests; though anyone can see that she doesn't really mind. Mrs. Pilling is the youngest of the mothers: an attractive woman, not yet forty. She still seems slightly dazed at being a widow. She inherited Mr. Pilling's shares in the firm, though they probably aren't worth much now. I suspect that she wouldn't be sorry if in a few years' time Sylvia and I confirmed the business link between our families with a personal one.

"She's gone off for a walk by herself," says Sylvia's brother Brian.

"By herself, eh?" Mr. Fox turns to me. "You're neglecting her, lad! You want to watch out, or she'll be finding herself a handsome young fisherman."

That remark is much less to Mrs. Pilling's liking than the other. Though she knows it's a joke, she purses her lips slightly. But nothing more is said. The straggly line of laden people stumbles and slithers down the track from our group of bungalows to the North Bay beach.

The mothers are anxious to get everything organized in the chalet. They shoo the rest of us away. Stumps are set up in the middle of a broad expanse of sand, so that Brian Pilling, the fathers, Paula, and I can play cricket. Rodney Fox and his sister Brenda decline.

Brian is the chief sporting enthusiast. He's fifteen: an eager, good-looking boy, cheerful and even-tempered. He is not only capable at games but absurdly keen on them, and can recite the professional football and cricket league tables from memory. With only five players you can't set up a cricket match; but Father and I bowl alternately, Brian bats with great style and aplomb, and Paula fields, while red-faced Mr. Fox takes it easy as wicket-keeper.

And after ten minutes I am bored, bored, bored with cricket on the beach. When next it's my turn to bowl, I hand over to Paula and sidle away, hoping nobody will say anything. And nobody does. I go and squat on the sand between Rodney and Brenda Fox. Rodney looks up briefly from his book, says "Hello, Phil," and goes on reading. Brenda shows more interest.

Brenda Fox is fifteen: dark, round-faced, pleasantly plump, with a bust that is distractingly well developed for her age. She is inclined to giggle and to speak in a little-girl voice; but this is deceptive, because she is actually rather mature. Brenda is amiable and obliging. I rather like her, and suspect that she rather likes me.

"It's a lovely day, Phil," she says.

I nod.

"Just think, five lovely weeks ahead of us. I hope it stays like this."

I nod again.

"You soon got tired of the cricket."

"Yes."

"We'll have to find some other things to do, won't we?"

"Who's 'we'?" I ask, a shade churlishly.

"Well, all of us," she says. "You know. The gang. You and Paula, and Rodney and me, and Sylvia and Brian."

"What other things *are* there to do?"

"Well, p'raps we can all go into Eastpool sometimes. There's lots to do there. Daddy'll lend us his car, I'm sure, if Rodney drives."

"If Rodney *feels* like driving," says Rodney, looking up.

"Oh, he will, Phil. He's not as mean as he makes out."

"I might be even meaner," says Rodney.

[23]

And suddenly I'm bored again. I don't want to play games on the beach, I don't really want to go into East-pool with the gang. I feel with a dreadful intensity that the yearly joint holiday of the three families has outlived its appeal. It was all right when we were all children, content to romp on the beach together. But now, apart from my small sister Alison, we are in our middle or later teens, and developing different interests. My elder sister Paula is eighteen and is only here because her plans to go abroad with a friend have fallen through. Rodney is going to university in the autumn, and has told me he's come to Linley to do some reading in peace and quiet. Brian and Brenda, at fifteen, now strike me as terribly young. We're not a gang; we're just an assortment.

There's Sylvia, of course. But I don't quite like the way things are going. Everybody seems to be getting the wrong idea about me and Sylvia. . . .

The only thing I really want to do at Linley is sail. I've been out a few times on an inland lake with a boy who owns a dinghy, but I want especially to sail on the sea. The sea is not land, the sea is elsewhere, the sea is a new element to move upon. I want to assert myself over wind and water.

And now: no boat. Not only no boat, but a quarrel with my father which lies heavily on my conscience. I've apologized, but I feel I've hurt his feelings in a way that an apology can't really cure.

And then of course there's Hitler.

I get to my feet.

"I'm going for a walk," I say.

"All by yourself?" Brenda asks.

"Yes."

"Are you"—her voice is very light—"going to look for Sylvia?"

"No."

"Don't interrogate him," Rodney tells her. "A man has a right to go off on his own if he feels like it." His eyes return to his book.

I set off along the cliff path that leads to Linley Bottom. It's rather a nice path. It passes to seaward of the Imperial Hotel, which stands in stone magnificence on its ridge between North Bay and the village. From the path's highest point, on a clear blue day like this, you can see right across the bay to Eastpool in one direction and to the Craven Head lighthouse in the other. It's a splendid view. There's a light, mild breeze. I ought to be happy, but . . .

I don't know what to do with myself between now and lunchtime, maybe an hour and a half. I walk along a little farther, downward now, to the point where the cliff path curves inward and transforms itself into Upper Row, the first of the Linley Bottom alleyways.

And at least I know what I can do to begin with. I will do what one always does at the start of a summer visit to Linley. I'll make my way along the East Cliff and see what's gone over the edge since last time we were here.

3

The sea is eating Linley. It's said that in the last two centuries three hundred houses have gone down the cliff. That's as many houses as now remain.

Unless a coastal defense plan is approved, there is no end in sight to the process. By the end of this century the last of the old village inns—humbly named the Fo'c'sle—will have gone. Fifty years or so after that the main street will be breached. Then the sea will start gnawing at the churchyard, claiming at last the bones of those generations of seafarers who escaped it in their lifetime. The sea is always hungry. By the year 2200 it will have finished its meal. The Imperial Hotel and North Bay will remain. But not a stick or stone of the original village will be left.

I walk along Upper Row, thinking of Ben Billington. Ben belonged to one of the old Linley fishing families, and was an amiable old chap, though not picturesque; in his retirement he preferred a serge suit to a fisherman's jersey. He always declared that he would die in the house where he was born. And he managed it with a week to spare. He died in his bed, aged seventy-nine. On the day of the funeral his cottage cracked apart. Three days later its wreckage was on the beach, sixty feet below the spot where it had stood since 1620. With it went Ben's worldly goods; his splintered furniture was mostly retrieved for firewood; he owned nothing else but the penny-a-week insurance policy that buried him. Ben will be remembered, if only for the timing of his death. There's a sentence about it in the local guidebook.

Now, in the summer of 1939, it's Middle Row which is in the front line. The house behind Ben's has gone, and the one next to it as well. And jutting out to sea are three small square stone houses which form a curious little peninsula. Temporarily perhaps they are supported by their stout and deep foundations, which are now exposed at each side, for the sea has taken nibbles to the left and right of them.

They will go, of course; it's only a matter of time. They are all empty and boarded up. The nearest one has been empty for some years; the second, if my memory is correct, was occupied until a few months ago by the Bergs, another old Linley family. The third, last and most distant is the most intriguing. It is spick and span; its doors and window frames have been painted in bright colors more recently than was really sensible. It does not look ready to die. I know that it is in fact a holiday cottage, belonging to two of the earliest of the summer people: a Mr. and Mrs. Partington, now elderly, who come from somewhere near Manchester. They can probably afford to lose their investment. They are rumored to be well-to-do.

Looking at this cottage, I feel a sudden urge to get into it. There is no explanation for this; it's just something that comes over me. Alongside the row of three is a remaining fringe of pathway, possibly two feet wide. Below it is the beach, and the beach is a long way down. And my head for heights is not too good. But I want to get into the Partingtons' cottage. I must get into the Partingtons' cottage.

I do not think the fringe of pathway will crumble. I know, or think I know, how erosion works at this point. I know, or think I know, that nothing will happen until there has been heavy rain to soak through and make the land unstable; until this instability has combined with a rough sea and high tide to bring the cliff sliding down and expose a further stretch. Today is calm, bright, dry; the sea is blue, harmless, far out; the beach glistens, clean and pale. But the palms of my hands are damp.

I am edging past the front of the first cottage; past a boarded window, a boarded doorway; I hold and grope my way around a downspout that now spouts on to nothing. I pass the second cottage. And it looks as though I cannot reach the third after all, for the thin strip of path degenerates; it slopes away from the wall; the soil is loose and gravelly, and if I step on it I shall slip and be lost.

I shall slip . . . but not perhaps be lost. With immense effort, holding at bay a dizziness that will drown my brain if I let it in, I look down and see that just below me is a jag of projecting masonry. Beside it, sticking out at a weird angle, is a young tree, still alive and half rooted; with its help I can keep a foothold. Now I am slithering downward; but I am not going to fall. I am poised for a moment on a bit of old wall; I half jump, half slip; and there is stone under my feet, and I am in what used to be a tiny paved area adjoining the basement of the Partingtons' cottage, now exposed to the air. I stagger inside, feeling weak in the legs, thinking I must be mad, wondering how—having got here—I shall ever get away again.

[28]

Upward from the basement, inside the cottage, leads a flight of stone steps. I sit on the bottom stair for a while, getting back my breath and my self-possession. When I've recovered I climb the steps and emerge into the kitchen above.

Strange; the little kitchen is fully equipped. Here is the gas cooker, shining white; here the refrigerator; here the neat sliding-doored cupboards, the enamel-topped kitchen table with a wringer built into it. It is all modern and expensive-looking. Well, everyone knew the Partingtons had money. But why is it all still here; why is not the cottage stripped like other doomed cottages?

I walk into the adjoining room: a sitting room. A sofa, armchairs, a carpet, a deep-pile rug. On a side table, an old-fashioned phonograph, and a large polished-walnut radio set. I switch the radio on, but nothing happens; I switch it off again.

Upstairs, two bedrooms; one double, one single, both furnished and carpeted. A bathroom and w.c., shining white. No water in the w.c. and no resistance when I pull the chain; but a large enameled water jug standing beside it, full.

I go downstairs again. I have a strong sense of trespass. I feel the owners will come back at any moment. My legs are still a little weak. I sit at the kitchen table. I am guilty and I am apprehensive. There is something eerie about this place.

Strange, strange, strange.

Not strange that a neat suburban interior has been forced into the shell of a centuries-old cottage. That has been done at Linley many times. But strange that all this equipment, these carpets are still here when the cottage is under death sentence, poised on the brink. Already there are vertical cracks in some of the walls, though they're narrow and not too noticeable. Whatever happens, the cottage cannot last through next winter. Given bad weather, it might go at any time.

And there is something even stranger. It does not dawn on me for some minutes what it is, for I am still a little dazed. Then I run my finger across the kitchen table. No dust. I look down at the quarry-tiled floor. No dust.

I open the refrigerator. It is not cold inside; there is no electricity. But there is food in it. Two or three grease-proof paper packages, some tomatoes, part of a chicken on a plate. I lift it out, put it to my nose. It smells wholesome. I put it back.

There is only one explanation. The Partingtons have been here recently and are coming back. They have still to move their furniture and equipment. They have left it pretty late, but no doubt they will be getting on with the job now.

For the moment this satisfies me. I even feel a recurrence of my uneasiness about trespassing. They may come in any minute and find me here.

Then once more, belatedly, my mind works. The Partingtons will come back? *How* will they come back? The Partingtons are elderly. They cannot scramble into their house as I have scrambled into it. And neither they nor anyone else can get anything out of here, ever again.

I walk into the tiny hallway and turn the handle of the front door. It does not open. Of course not. It is locked, bolted, and boarded up from outside; and anyway, both door and frame are slightly askew from subsidence. And if one did open it, it would open on to nothing.

Nobody is going to come through that door again.

This is a ghost house. I am nervous, and my heart is bumping a bit. It is time I looked for a way to safety. If I cannot get back the way I came, what will happen? Sooner or later I shall be able to attract somebody's notice, and no doubt I can be got out with ropes and ladders. They won't have to call the Eastpool fire brigade. But I shall feel silly, very silly. And with a man like Mr. Fox around, it will be a long time before I hear the last of it.

Then there is a scrabbling sound. I jump.

It comes from the back of this little hallway. There is a cupboard under the stairs, an ordinary broom cupboard. I look towards it. Rats? Could be, I suppose, but I don't think so. I don't like it.

There can't be a *person* in the cupboard?

The door opens from inside. I open my mouth and let out breath, the silent edge of a scream. I feel the whiteness of my face.

A girl steps from the cupboard. She doesn't see me at first, because I am in shadow and don't move. She turns, closes the door behind her. Then she turns again and catches sight of me. She gives a little cry, quickly cut off. And then she is scrambling back into the cupboard.

The door closes behind her. I step forward and jerk it open again. She is just opening the back of the cupboard, and there is light beyond it. It communicates with the next house.

Now I understand. In Linley this is not a mystery, it is a commonplace. The village is riddled with escape routes. They date from smuggling days. It's said that a man who was sought by the preventive officers could move through the village in any of a dozen directions, from house to house or through underground tunnels, and come out at any point that wasn't guarded. False cupboards are frequent in Linley Bottom. Some have been closed up, some haven't. Some owners are proud of them.

I catch the girl's wrist.

"Come out!" I tell her, and she comes.

She is more frightened than I am; much more, for I am recovering rapidly. I can see at once that she has nothing to do with the Partingtons; that she has no right to be here, any more than I have. I attack.

"Who are you?" I demand. "What are you doing here?"

She doesn't say anything. I drag her through to the kitchen and pull out a chair from under the table.

"Sit there," I say. "Don't try to run away. Now, I asked you a question. What are you doing here?"

She is trembling.

"Are you—are you one of them?" she asks. "I mean, the people. The people who own it?"

"What do you think I am?" I try to sound like an outraged owner. "Why, I've a good mind to . . ."

Then I stop. I'm not such a bully as that. I haven't the heart to go on.

The girl is about my age, though at first glance she looks younger. She is thin, small-boned, two or three inches shorter than I am, her figure hardly developed at all. She wears a white blouse, a navy blue divided skirt, and gym shoes. The effect is childish. But her face is less childish than the rest of her. It is pale, the forehead fairly broad, the chin narrow. Her hair is dark, her eyes large and gray. She is not pretty.

I laugh.

"You're trespassing, aren't you?" I say. "So am I."

I laugh again. The girl looks at me wide-eyed and says nothing.

"What's your name?" I ask.

"Ann."

"Ann what?"

"Tarrant." Very quietly. Then silence.

"I'm Philip Martin."

[32]

Still she says nothing. She sits motionless, her hands clasped, without nervous gesture, but still tense. Her eyes, wide, are still on mine.

I notice on her wrist the red mark of my own grip.

"I'm sorry about that," I say. I lean across the table, put out my own hand. "Let me look." But she draws her hand away.

I don't quite know what to say, because her silence and withdrawal are disconcerting. But I am feeling more relaxed all the time. I am not shy with girls; I tend to assume they'll like me.

"Do you live here?" I ask.

Her eyes move from mine. Momentarily she looks around her.

"Not exactly," she says.

"I didn't mean right here in this house," I say. I smile at the absurdity of the thought, but it sticks in a corner of my mind all the same. "I meant in Linley Bottom."

"You could say so," she says after some thought. "As much as anywhere."

"You don't sound local," I tell her. To me her accent seems faintly Cockney.

"I'm at the Imperial Hotel," she says.

"You mean you *live* at the Imperial?" I am surprised. The Imperial is expensive; its guests are monied people. It would cost a lot to live there permanently.

"My mother works there. On the reception desk. We have a room. It's not very grand. Practically an attic."

"And your father?" I ask; and realize at once that this is a tactless question.

She frowns slightly and says, "He isn't with us."

Silence again. She has hardly taken her eyes from mine. She has answered my questions, but she doesn't ask me

[33]

any. I feel that she looks on herself as my prisoner. I smile, but she doesn't respond.

"Who keeps this place so neat and tidy?" I ask.

"I do."

"Why? Who *for?*"

"Not for anybody, really. I just—well, I sort of like to do it."

"It's a bit pointless, isn't it?"

"Perhaps."

"You said you didn't live here *exactly*. As if you meant this very place. What were you getting at? Did you mean you have it as a kind of—a kind of—"

For a moment I am stuck, because I can't find a word for the idea I want to express. Then a word from childish games comes to mind.

"A kind of den?" I finish.

At last, faintly, she smiles; the merest glimmer of a smile.

"You could call it that."

"And you come here by yourself?"

"Yes."

"And nobody else knows about it?"

"I don't think so. Anyway, nobody else comes."

"But how do you *get* here?"

"Oh, that's easy. Through the cupboards. There's a false cupboard to every house in this row. You just have to look around for them."

"But . . . I still don't really understand. How did you ever come to be looking for them?"

"Exploring," she says. "I explore a lot. Or I used to, until I found this. Now I don't explore so much. I come here. Are you going to tell anyone?"

"Why should I? It's nobody else's business. Except the

Partingtons, who own the cottage. And if they don't want you here, they can tell you so themselves."

"You see," the girl says, "for me it's a sort of—well, it's a sort of home. If you know what I mean."

A pause.

"Are you staying at the hotel?" she asks. This is the first question she has put to me, and I am glad.

"No," I say. "We have a cottage here. But I know the hotel. Sometimes we get friendly with visitors there, and play tennis on the hard courts."

"You wouldn't get to know *us*. We're only staff. At least, my mother's staff. I'm not anything at all. And an hotel—well, it's a good hotel, I know it's a good hotel, and they treat us all right, but an hotel's not a home, is it?"

"I suppose not."

She is gaining confidence, growing readier to talk.

"And my mother's working, of course," she goes on. "And when she's not working she's often . . . well, busy. I have plenty of time to myself. And now I have this."

"Your home," I say. "And now you have a visitor. Me. Am I the first?"

"You are the first," she says gravely. She goes on, in a formal manner which is put on deliberately but which somehow doesn't seem too far from the natural.

"I'm glad you've come." A very small smile. "May I offer you a cup of tea?"

It is a game, and I enter into it.

"That would be delightful, Miss—er—"

"Tarrant." She is very grave now.

"Miss Tarrant. Thank you so much. A cup of tea would be most refreshing."

Then I forget, and say, "Can you really make tea here?"

[35]

"Not really," she says. "There's no gas or electricity. But I've some lemonade in the cupboard. We can have it in a cup, and pretend."

I look at her with half a grin.

"I pretend all the time," she says, in a small, apologetic voice. Then, in the formal tones again, "Perhaps you'd care to go into the drawing room?"

I go into the adjoining room. Its main window is boarded up. But there's a smaller window in the end wall, looking out across the bay. I step over to it, and at first sight there's nothing in front of me but the blue of sea and sky. I put my face close to the pane and look down, and there's the beach below, and the eaten face of the cliff curving away to it. We are right on the edge.

The girl comes in with a tray.

"I can't think how I got here without falling," I say. "It's a wonder I didn't finish up as a nasty mess on the sand."

"I hoped you would come," the girl says. "I've been wishing for someone to come who would understand. I wished very hard. I think I must have magic powers."

"But when you saw me you were frightened."

"Yes, I was frightened. Well, it might have been the owners. And even if it wasn't the owners, I wasn't sure that I wanted somebody coming into my secret place after all. Besides, I couldn't be certain it was the magic working. It might have been somebody horrible."

"I'm glad you don't think I'm horrible."

On the tray are biscuits, two teacups, a teapot. I watch as the girl pours lemonade from the pot into the two cups.

"We used to do that when we were small," I tell her. "Playing house. It was a *little* kids' game really, of course."

She looks at me reprovingly, but makes no comment.

[36]

"Do sit down," she says; and then, "I'm afraid I can't offer you milk or sugar."

We sit in armchairs opposite each other.

"It's a very fine day, Mr.—er—Martin, is it not?"

I look at the two teacups, full of lemonade, and burst out laughing. Her face quivers. For a moment I think she is going to laugh, too, but she doesn't. I try hard to recover.

"Yes, Miss Tarrant. Or may I—" I can only splutter now. "May I call you Ann?"

"That is a little presumptuous, sir," she says severely. But now she in turn is unable to keep it up. We sit laughing at each other, then trying to stop, then catching each other's eye and laughing afresh. When I think I have sobered down I pick up my cup, but the sight of the lemonade, masquerading as tea, sets me off again. I put it down hastily before it spills.

When at last we have calmed down sufficiently to drink from our cups the girl says, "Do you know, Philip, I'm really very shy?"

That is obvious enough. But I feel inclined to tease her.

"Shy?" I say. "Come off it. Hobnobbing like this with a total stranger. The word I'd use is 'brazen.'"

I am ready for us both to laugh again, but she's looking troubled, as though her own remark had disconcerted her. I go to the window again.

"It feels perilous here," I say. "Aren't you ever afraid?"

"No, I'm never frightened. At least, not of things like that. The things I'm frightened of are . . . different."

I think now I can see fear in her face. And suddenly I know that, for the present, I've stayed long enough. It would be inconsiderate to linger. She needs time to collect herself.

Anyway, I ought perhaps to be going. I glance at my

[37]

watch. Twelve noon. Yes, I had better start making my way back to North Bay.

I return to the formal manner.

"Miss Tarrant, I fear I have an engagement elsewhere. I must take my leave. May I say how delighted I am to have made your acquaintance?"

I bow.

"The pleasure, sir, is all mine," she says.

"I trust I may call again."

Her face is too expressive for her own good. All in a second I can see alarm, doubt, hope, pleasure.

"That would be delightful, Mr. Martin." And reverting at once to her everyday voice with that faint touch of Cockney, she goes on, "I'll show you how to get out of here."

She goes ahead of me. It is really quite simple. Each house in the row has, as she said, a concealed communicating door with the next. At the innermost house in the row we go up to the floor above and round a narrow corridor. Now we're in a dusty lumber-room which is part of a bridge over the next alleyway. We go down steps at the other side and are in yet another empty cottage. There's a way through into an outhouse, with a standpipe, a hose, buckets, old garden tools.

"I get water here," Ann says. "That tap still works."

The outhouse door is stiff, but opens to a good tug. Beyond it is a yard full of flowerpots, hundreds of flowerpots. Most are in stacks, empty, but a few have soil in them and some contain stunted plants, struggling to live. And there are hanging baskets like outsize birds' nests; they hold the miniature gardens of yesteryear, mostly dead, but again with a few signs of life. Everything seems abandoned, forgotten.

Ann peers through a knothole in the yard gate, then

unlatches it. We slip through and are in yet another alley-way.

"Do you know where we are?" she asks.

"More or less."

"It's Lower Row. Go straight along till you come to the main street. Turn left for the village, right for the Imperial."

She makes to slip back through the yard gate.

"Can I come tomorrow?" I ask.

She hesitates, but her face is saying yes.

"What time?" I press her.

She doesn't answer. Now she is glancing nervously up and down the alley, although nobody is coming and there is not a sound.

"I'll come in the morning if I can. You'll be here in the morning, won't you?"

"I might," she says, and is gone.

4

I pass the main gate of the Imperial Hotel, rejoin the cliff path, and head towards North Bay. I've just reached the highest point of the path when I feel a tap on my left shoulder. I turn, and there is no one there. I hear Sylvia's laugh. She has passed me quietly on the right, and played the old childish trick of touching me on the wrong side.

"Hello, Phil," she says.

"Hello, Syl."

Ahead of us and below on the beach we can see small moving figures. They look like the members of our party.

"Why aren't you with the rest of them?" Sylvia asks.

"I could ask you the same."

"Oh, because," she says.

"Because what?"

"Just because."

A smile comes and goes at the corners of her mouth.

"Secrets?" I ask.

"Maybe."

Sylvia is always cheerful, but today she is more than cheerful. She is happy; she bubbles with excitement.

"Tell me," I say.

"Why should I?"

"Why shouldn't you?"

"It mightn't be any of your business."

"Oh, well, I can guess," I tell her.

"Go on, then. Guess."

"You met a boy."

"Brilliant," she says. "I think I'll call you Sherlock." And then, contentedly, "Yes, I met a boy."

"He must be something special. Because he's not the first boy you've ever met. Or the second or the third. . . ."

"All right, that'll do," she says. Then, dreamily, "Yes, he's special."

"Do I know him?"

"Yes, you do."

"Who?"

"I don't know whether I'm going to tell you. I haven't decided yet."

"I'll find out."

"You might. You might not."

"Well, give me a clue."

"It's not somebody I've just met today. I met him when we were here earlier in the year. And I met him last year and the year before. But I didn't know then whether he liked me, and he didn't know whether I liked him."

"And now you find you do. Now you find you're daft about each other."

"That's right," she says. She smiles again, happily.

I try to think of boys I know among the other summer visitors, but can't think of one who seems likely to appeal to Sylvia.

"Mother won't like it, though," she says. "Mother won't like it at all."

She looks at me ruefully, the smile fading from her lips.

"Aha! Somebody your mother wouldn't approve of! That sounds interesting."

We are nearer now to our own party, and they can recognize us. Somebody waves from the beach and we wave back. Just ahead of us, beside the path, is a boulder which we all sometimes sit on.

"Sit down here a minute, will you, Phil?" Sylvia says.

She rests her chin on her hand, gazing abstractedly out to sea.

"The Thinker," I say.

For a moment there's silence. Then Sylvia asks, "What were you doing this morning, Phil?"

"Oh, just wandering around."

"On your own?"

"Partly."

"I just wondered . . . Phil, you wouldn't by any chance have been seeing a girl?"

For some reason the question takes me by surprise.

"Well . . . Well, yes, I suppose I have, sort of."

" 'Sort of'? Goodness, Phil, don't you *know?*"

"All right, then, yes, I have."

"Are you planning to see her again?"

"I suppose I might."

Another brief silence. Then Sylvia says, "Phil, what do you feel about *me?*"

I stare.

"What do you mean?"

"You know what I mean. Well, you know what everybody *thinks*, don't you?"

"Yes. They think we're . . . They think it's . . ."

"They think it's love's young dream, don't they? But it isn't, is it, Phil? Honestly, now?"

I find this slightly embarrassing.

"Well, no, I suppose not. I mean, I've always liked you, Syl, and we get on well together. But it just isn't like that. It's—I was going to say it's like brother and sister, but it isn't, it's better, because you and I don't have rows like I do with Paula. It's—well, I suppose we're *friends*."

"Thank you, Phil," she says. "That's how I feel, too. But if I try to suggest it to my mother, she doesn't understand. Perhaps she doesn't really want to understand."

"Perhaps not. Do you know, Syl, Mr. Fox this morning referred to you as my sweetheart. And you should have seen your mother's face. She liked it. I'm sure she was hearing wedding bells already."

"Oh, dear, oh, dear." Sylvia pulls a face of comic dismay. "The trouble is, you're so *suitable*."

"You're suitable, too."

We are both laughing.

"But she wasn't so pleased," I go on, "when Mr. Fox said I'd better watch out or you'd be finding yourself a handsome young fisherman. Your mother didn't like *that* at all."

Sylvia jerks up straight and shoots a sharp look at me. "Whatever made him say that?"

"Oh, I don't know. Just joking, I expect."

"It's a funny kind of joke. . . . You know, Phil, I think I shall run into trouble. She *will* be awkward, there's no doubt about it. If she finds out, she'll probably take me straight home or lock me up or send me to a convent or something."

Sylvia ponders for a moment. Then she says, "Listen, Phil, I have an idea. Why don't we let them all go *on*

[43]

thinking we're wild about each other? Then we can go off together pretty well as often as we like. And when we're away from the crowd we can go our own ways."

"Syl!" I am surprised and rather shocked. "Sylvia Pilling! I wouldn't have thought you had so much low cunning in you!"

"It's a kindness to Mother, really," she says, straight-faced. "I'm just trying to save her from worrying."

We both laugh again. I find the idea attractive. There's a neatness in the deception that is rather pleasing. I have pangs of conscience, but put them aside.

"Won't they soon find out?" I ask.

"I don't think so. They wouldn't spy on us, would they?"

"No, I'm sure they wouldn't."

"And how often do they go into the village?"

"Not often. It's a steep walk up and down, and you're not allowed to take a car into Main Street because it's so narrow. They go in as far as Mrs. Billington's shop occasionally, that's all."

"Well, then, if we're careful we'll be all right."

"But how often are we going to do this?" I ask.

"Not all day and every day. My—my friend can't. The next three or four days I can only see him mornings. Then it'll change."

"Oh, Sylvia, Sylvia. You're a terrible creature and you're leading me into wicked ways. But all right, seeing it's you, I'll do it."

"Good old Phil. I knew you would. Now get ready for the rest of the day on the beach, and be thankful it's fine."

We get up and continue towards North Bay. Sylvia is bubbling again.

"Oh, I feel so *good,*" she says. "I feel so wonderful, just being alive." She throws an imaginary tennis ball into the

[44]

air and hits it with an imaginary racquet. "There, you never even *saw* that service," she says. "Game, set, and match to me, six-love, six-love."

"Don't kid yourself!"

"I'll give you a game this evening and beat you all ends up."

"Oh, yes?"

"Oh, yes, yes, yes. And now, come on, Phil. Everybody's left the beach. They'll all be having lunch in the chalet."

We run together down the last quarter-mile of the path. There is a tiny round of applause when we appear, hand in hand.

"Here come the lovebirds," says Mr. Fox.

Brenda looks at me with slight reproach. I remember that I said I wasn't going to look for Sylvia, and now I've come back with her after all. Oh, well, that's just too bad. If anything, it will help the deception.

"You're just in time for lunch," my mother says. "Where have you both been?"

"Perhaps we shouldn't ask them that," says Mr. Fox. He winks broadly.

"Bernie, please!" says Mrs. Fox in a warning tone.

I can see that it's going to be easy.

5

Friday the fourth of August. Another sunny morning. I call at the Pillings' for Sylvia. Mrs. Pilling is delighted to see me. Brian isn't quite so pleased.

"I suppose you two are off again," he says.

"I suppose so."

Brian sighs.

"I'd hoped we'd do more things together," he says. "I didn't realize that you and Sylvia were going to be like *that*."

"Brian, dear," Mrs. Pilling says, "I don't think you understand. The time hasn't come for you yet, but it will. The time when somebody seems rather *special,* and you want to be with them more than anybody else."

A groan from Brian.

"Cheer up," I tell him. "Sylvia and I aren't all *that* exclusive. We were on the beach with you yesterday afternoon."

"But you're not coming on tomorrow's excursion, are you?"

"Well, no. But that's only one outing. Think of all the swimming and sunbathing we're going to do in the next few weeks."

"If it keep fine," says Brian, "and Hitler doesn't start something. Rodney says it might be any day now."

He brightens a little, all the same.

"I suppose old Syl had to be sweet on *somebody*," he says philosophically, "and it might as well be you."

I report this to Sylvia a few minutes later as we set off along the cliff path to the village. She laughs.

"I told you we were suitable," she says. "Even Brian thinks we're suitable for each other."

Sylvia is happy again. She sings snatches from popular songs; sings them tunefully, for among all her gifts from nature is a good singing voice. When we near Middle Row I drop back to let her go ahead. Sylvia looks about her with mild interest; but she is too eager to be on her way to show much curiosity.

I find the cottage with the walled yard, and let myself in. The yard is still full of flowerpots, elderly garden tools, boxes and baskets of mainly-dead plants with a few straggly survivors; and the back door of the house still opens to a determined shove. I close it behind me, find my way into the next cottage, then cross over the archway through the house that bridges it, and descend at the other side. I go through the false cupboards—it is all very simple—and am in the Partingtons' cottage.

Everything is clean and tidy, but there is no Ann. This ought not to surprise me, but it does. And I am surprised by my own disappointment.

I cross to the seaward window. Nothing has changed. The sea is sunshine blue, with darker patches where rocks lurk under water. A steamship crawls along the horizon, slowly, slowly. I look down and am horrified once more

[47]

by the immediate downward swoop of the cliff face. I move away from the window, and permanence re-establishes itself. This is a house; an equipped, habitable house; and houses last forever. I sit down and wait.

A quarter-hour passes; half an hour. I am bored. She is not coming. I wonder what I shall do from now until lunchtime. I wonder what I shall do tomorrow, when the whole party except Sylvia and myself is going on a full-day excursion to Craven Head lighthouse and Four Mile Beach beyond.

Outside, a fine morning is being lost from my life. I drum with my fingers; look at my watch more and more often. At last I have had enough. I get up, make my way back by the same route, jerk open the door that leads into the flowerpot-filled back yard. And am looking into her eyes.

She steps back, alarmed, then embarrassed. All around are the stacks of flowerpots, the boxes and baskets of most-ly-dead plants.

"I was watering plants," she says apologetically. "I do it sometimes. You see, some of them are still alive."

"You knew I was here?" I ask.

"I—well, I didn't *know,* but I guessed you might be."

I laugh.

"Do you know what you made me think of? Somebody hovering on the dentist's doorstep, trying to pluck up courage."

She says nothing. Her face is pink.

"Don't worry," I tell her. "I'm not going to pull your teeth out."

She shudders.

"You were afraid again, weren't you?"

Her eyes beg me to let it drop, but I don't.

"You soon stopped being afraid yesterday. There's no

reason to start again today. I'm only a human being. Just Philip. You remember, don't you? It's silly looking so scared."

Then it dawns on me that I'm bullying her again. I don't want to do that. I smile and try to recapture the formal tone we used before.

"It is a pleasure, madam, to renew our acquaintance."

"The pleasure is mutual, sir," she says gravely.

At last we both smile.

"Well," I say, "Here we are, anyway. What would you like to do? Are we going into the happy home?"

"I think—I think I'd rather not. That is, if you don't mind."

"*I* don't mind. Just as you wish. Shall we go for a walk?"

"Yes," she says. "I'd like that. I'm supposed to go for long walks. They're good for me."

"You're not frightened of me now, are you?"

"No." She smiles again, still a little uncertainly.

"Let's go down to the Bottom," I suggest, "and round to South Bay."

"All right."

"I don't want to meet my family or our friends." I wonder if I should try to explain my arrangement with Sylvia, but it seems too complicated and might even alarm her. And she asks no questions.

"I'll take you my way down," she says. "Then you won't meet *anybody*."

"You have a special way?"

"Very special. I told you I do a lot of exploring."

We go back as far as the cottage that spans the archway. But instead of going upstairs towards the arch, Ann leads me down into the basement. And from a dark corner of the basement, steps go on downwards into a tunnel. It's

[49]

dark at this end of it, but only a few yards along there's blue sky, and light shining in. The passage comes out into the cliff face.

"It must have gone farther at one time," says Ann, "before so much of the cliff fell away."

But I don't need telling that. Everyone knows that Linley Bottom is riddled with tunnels. A few broad ones, for smuggled goods. Many narrow ones, for escaping smugglers.

On our right, just before we come out into the cliff face, is the blocked-up opening of another passage.

"That probably goes down to the Bottom," I say. "If so, it's been filled in all the way along. They filled in lots of tunnels a few years ago, for safety's sake. And do you know, Harold Ericson told me, in one place they found two skeletons, together? And one of them had a marlin-spike through its skull."

"Ugh."

"And somewhere else they found a cask of brandy. Full."

"Was it drinkable?"

"Well, they drank it."

Now we've come to the opening and are looking seaward once more. And suddenly I'm uneasy. There's a way down to the shore, but it's the tiniest of paths, only like a sheep track, running diagonally down the cliff face.

"You've a good head for heights, haven't you?" Ann asks.

"Well . . ."

"You must have, or you wouldn't have got round the outside of the cottages the way you did. That's dangerous; this isn't."

She goes ahead of me, running lightly along the track. I don't have time to explain that actually my head for heights is poor, and that the surroundings affect me more than the actual degree of danger. To me, this one is nastier than edging my way round the row of houses. There isn't the reassuring familarity of walls, doors, windows; only the blank, uncrannied face of the cliff. I follow, perspiring, trying to plant my feet firmly at each step, trying above all not to look down, in terror of the invading dizziness. It feels like a reprieve when at last the beach is near and I can run without fear along the last few descending yards of the track.

I arrive long after Ann, with sweat standing on my forehead. I am humbled; my feeling of strength and superiority in contrast with her nervousness has evaporated. I grin in relief and apology. She knows; she must know; but she doesn't say anything.

It only takes us five minutes to walk along the shore, round the foot of East Cliff, to the Bottom. The Bottom is where Linley village comes down to the water. It lies at the head of an inlet where, at low tide, a small sandy beach is exposed. There is no harbor, but there's a slipway, used mainly by the Ericsons, last of the Linley fishermen.

Overlooking the beach is Bottom Square, the lowest point of the village, into which the long straggling main street descends. Bottom Square rests on a massive stone structure—a fortress against the sea—and under the Square is the Cavern, part natural, part man-made. Usually the Cavern holds an overspill of boats and gear from the boathouse on the Square above.

This morning, as Ann and I walk past, we can see that three or four boats are drawn up inside the open entrance to the Cavern, above high-water mark. One of these interests me, and I wander across. I cannot see it too clearly in the Cavern's half-light; but it is a smallish, clinker-built sailing boat. It is broad-beamed and looks slow and cumbersome, not like a modern racing dinghy; but it also looks stable and seaworthy.

"Do you like boats, Ann?" I ask.

"I don't know. I've hardly ever been in one."

"I expect these belong to the Ericsons."

The Ericsons. All the Ericsons are tall, blond, handsome. They are said to be of Viking blood, and look it. They have been in Linley for more centuries than the churchyard stones have record of. Their eldest sons are always called Harold. Now, in summer at any rate, they are boatmen more than fishermen. Harold Ericson the nineteenth is a year or two older than I am. His father is away in the Merchant Navy, but his grandfather, Harold Ericson the seventeenth, strong and active at nearly seventy, is down at the slipway every day and is very much in charge. He and Harold put out their lobster pots, and occasionally go netting salmon if conditions are right; but mostly their livelihood comes from boat hire or from fishing trips for visitors, charged by the hour.

Ann and I move out of the Cavern and continue on our way. We have to cross the slipway. As we do so, I look up towards Bottom Square. Sitting on the low wall at its seaward edge, with their backs towards us, are two people. One is a blue-jerseyed figure with cropped, tow-colored hair. This is Harold Ericson, grown broader since last I saw him. He is mending nets. Beside him, leaning towards him, is a girl. A girl whose hair is as fair as his own.

Sylvia.

I think at once of Mr. Fox's remark about a handsome young fisherman. Had he seen something? No, I'm sure he hadn't. It was joking. Or prophetic.

I wonder whether to go up into the Square and speak to them, but glance sideways at Ann and decide against it.

It could embarrass her, or Sylvia, or all of us. I say nothing. We walk on towards South Bay. While we're in view from the Square I feel uncomfortable, as if we were in an exposed position; but when we've picked our way between the rocks and are away from Linley I relax.

"Hello, Ann," I say encouragingly.

The smile again, a little readier than before. A nice smile, but you still couldn't call her pretty. A shame.

"Hello, Philip," she says.

"I like it around here. Sort of up and down and round and round and interesting."

"Yes," she says. "And it's nice having it fine at last, when it's been so awful this summer."

I wonder if we are on the verge of another of those odd, formal, old-fashioned conversations. I suspect that they're a way of keeping a distance between us.

"Look, Ann," I say. "I don't know anything about you. Tell me."

"What do you want to know?" she asks. She is defensive again, her eyes troubled.

"Well, you know, just the ordinary things. Are you still at school?"

"I don't know," she says. "I don't think so."

"You don't *think* so?"

She takes a deep breath.

"It hasn't made any difference for quite a while," she says. "I've been in a sanatorium."

This silences me. In the 1930's the phrase has an alarming ring. It immediately suggests tuberculosis, and everyone is afraid of tuberculosis.

"It was pleurisy," she says. "I'm all right now. Still, I should have told you before."

I recover.

"You've not had much chance to tell me," I point out. "And did you think I'd take to my heels and run?"

[53]

"You wouldn't be the first person who did." She doesn't sound resentful. "Anyway, I suppose most of the summer I've been convalescing. That's why my mother took this job at the Imperial. It's healthy here, that's what they say. I'm supposed to take it easy and not strain myself and sit out when it's sunny. And I can go for walks in good weather, but I mustn't overdo it. Or swim, just yet. And I have to do breathing exercises in front of open windows. And now you know as much as I do. I haven't been to school since last winter, and I just don't know if I'll go back. I'd like to, but my mother thinks if I'm well enough I should be working, and you can't blame her, can you?"

"I suppose not."

"Well, you can't, truly. Not with my father being away. I could have got a job at the Imperial, but the doctor wouldn't hear of it, so she wasn't very pleased about that."

"Does she know what you do all day?"

"Not really. She . . . has other things to think about."

"You mean she doesn't care?"

That was a rude and silly thing to say, and Ann is distressed.

"No, I don't mean that. I mean . . . Why don't you tell me about *your* family?"

"Well," I begin, "I have a father and a mother and two sisters. One's eighteen and the other's only seven. And my father has a clothing factory, just a little one in a back street. And I go to a school that's four hundred years old, but it's a day school, not a boarding school. Not what you'd call superior. And we have a summer bungalow at North Bay, but we haven't come here often this year because the weather's been so awful. And that's about all."

"And you all live together at your own home?"

"Well, yes, of course."

"Is it, sort of, nice and comfortable and familyish?"

"I suppose so."

"How long have your father and mother been married?"

"Twenty years," I tell her. "It was their anniversary just before we came away."

"Do they still love each other?"

This is an impertinent question, but she asks it so simply and directly that it doesn't occur to me to take offense.

"I suppose so . . . Yes, I'm sure they do."

"That's nice." She sighs. "My father left my mother. He lives with somebody else."

There's nothing I can say about that, so I keep silent.

"He gives my mother a bit of money, but not much. So she has to work. And with me being ill this year, she hasn't had a very good time."

"It must be hard for her," I say. That seems safe enough.

"Yes, it is."

"They aren't divorced?"

"No. She wouldn't divorce him. Well, you can't blame her, can you? I mean, it would only have been for his convenience, it wouldn't have done *her* any good."

"Would it have done her any harm?"

"I don't know. Anyway, she may change her mind. She has a—a friend of her own now."

"Oh."

"You can't blame her," Ann says for the third time. I feel she has said it too often, and as if trying to persuade herself rather than me. "It's not very nice for her, on her own."

Then, with sudden passion, "If I loved a man, I'd love him forever and ever. And I'd want him to love me forever and ever. Or at least, as long as I lived."

[55]

I am startled. I stoop to pick up an oddly-shaped piece of driftwood.

"It looks like a horse's head," I say. "Doesn't it?"

"It does, rather. Or perhaps a giraffe. You see its long neck?"

But it's her earlier words that ring in my ears.

I throw the bit of driftwood down again. There's a breeze, light and warm. The shadow of a small cloud moves over Craven Head. Far out is a white sail. I think of the dinghy I'd hoped to have, and feel in my fingers the urge to hold a main sheet and a tiller.

We have come as far as we can get along the beach, but there's an easy way up the cliff. At the top, one path goes on towards Craven Head, the other back to the village.

"Which shall we take?" Ann asks.

"Perhaps we should be getting back. You're not supposed to overdo it, are you?"

"I'm all right," she says with a touch of impatience. But then she adds, "Thank you for thinking about it."

"Oh, I'm like that," I say, joking. "Thoughtful Philip, that's me." (It is untrue.)

"It's been a lovely morning," she says. "And the sun still shining. I thought it had forgotten how. But suddenly it seems to have remembered."

"Where do you want to go back to?" I ask.

"To the hotel."

"Not the cottage?"

"No. I have lunch at the hotel. With the staff. My mother arranged it."

"I thought I saw food in the cottage; that's why I asked."

"Yes, well, sometimes I do sort of picnic there. . . . Will I be seeing you tomorrow, Philip?"

"I don't see why not. Most of our lot are going to Four

[56]

Mile Beach, the other side of Craven Head, but they're not expecting me to go. Probably I'll be free all day."

"All day!" Ann says. Then, hesitantly, "Could we go for a picnic? Or—could we have a kind of picnic lunch in the cottage?"

"This morning I felt as if you didn't really want me to go in there."

She is embarrassed.

"I—I wasn't sure about things," she says. "It's such a private place. Some days I can't bear the thought of sharing it. Other times . . . oh, you wouldn't understand. Anyway, I feel I know you better now, and it's different."

"You're satisfied I won't do anything dreadful?"

"I never did think you'd do anything dreadful."

"Well, if you feel you can trust me, the answer's yes, please, I'd love to come."

"I should be honored to have your company, sir," she says in the formal manner.

I'm twenty minutes late at the point where I've arranged to meet Sylvia on the way back to lunch. When she is not there, I think she must have got tired of waiting and gone ahead. But I decide to give her five minutes, just in case. And before the five minutes have gone she arrives from the direction of Linley Bottom, unhurried, unthinking, happy.

"Have you been waiting long, Phil?" she asks.

"Ages and ages," I say untruthfully, hoping to put her at a disadvantage for future use.

"I'm ever so sorry."

But she isn't sorry at all. I see it all in her eyes. She couldn't care less.

"I know who your boyfriend is," I tell her.

"Oh?"

"It's Harold. The Last of the Vikings."

[57]

"Mmm."

She doesn't really mind my knowing. Yesterday she enjoyed having her little secret, but today she's just as ready to enjoy sharing it.

"Isn't he lovely?" she says; and adds, teasing me, "Much better-looking than you!"

"But much less suitable," I remind her, tongue in cheek.

"Oh, suitable, suitable!" says Sylvia. " 'I love my love with an S, because he is Suitable!' Not likely!"

Then she goes on, more soberly, "Still, you see my point about what Mother would say if she knew."

I see it all too clearly. Sylvia's father was quite well-known in his community, and since he died her mother has clung determinedly to her social position. She'd be appalled by the very idea of a friendship between her well-brought-up, well-spoken daughter and a jerseyed boatman. It's no use suggesting that Sylvia should introduce him and hope for the best. Not in 1939 it isn't. The result, if it were nothing worse, would be an immediate veto and constant supervision for the rest of the holiday.

"Can you really keep it from her?" I ask.

"I don't know. It's risky. But every day's a day gained. And we might not have many more. Ask Rodney."

We have arrived on North Beach, where lunch in the chalet is about to begin.

"Ask Rodney what?" says Rodney.

"How many days we have left."

Rodney pushes his newspaper across. POLES TELL HITLER, HANDS OFF DANZIG, says the main headline.

"War in a month at the outside," Rodney predicts. He looks at us with cynical benevolence.

" 'Gather ye rosebuds while ye may,' " he says.

6

"I'll come all the way with you this morning," I say to Sylvia. "I want to talk to Harold Ericson about a boat."

"All right," she says. Then, curious, "Are you still seeing this girl you told me about?"

"Later on. She's giving me lunch."

"That sounds promising."

"So you needn't worry. I won't stay with you too long."

"I don't mind," Sylvia says. "Harold and I can't go anywhere this morning anyway."

Down at the Bottom, Harold is doing something to an outboard motor. He turns towards us and wipes his hands on a rag. His eyes meet Sylvia's, but he doesn't say anything to her. To me he says, " 'Morning, sir."

The "sir" is not obsequious. It's casual, his usual way of addressing a prospective customer. All the same, it's a surprise, because I've known Harold since we were small boys, and we've always been on first-name terms.

"It's *Philip,* Harold," Sylvia says reprovingly. "You know Philip."

"Hello, Philip," says Harold. He grins but isn't quite at ease. He looks down at his hands, which are still black and oily.

"I was wondering about hiring a sailing boat," I tell him.

"Best go to Eastpool," says Harold promptly. "It's not so good for sailing, here at Linley. Hard to get in or out, if the wind and tide aren't right."

"But you do have a sailing boat, don't you?"

"Not for hiring," Harold says.

"I thought I saw one in the Cavern."

"Oh, you did, did you?" Harold looks at me rather hard.

"White, clinker-built, about fourteen foot," I tell him.

"*Seasprite,*" says Harold. "Yes, she's ours. Used to be my uncle's, down the coast, till he gave up." He ponders. "She's not been painted this year," he says. "And she'll leak a bit. I'm not so keen on getting her out."

"Oh, come on, Harold," says Sylvia. "Be helpful."

"You don't understand, miss."

"Miss!" repeats Sylvia indignantly. "Harold, for heaven's sake! Listen, Philip knows we're friends. You don't have to talk like that."

"You still don't understand," says Harold. "About boats, I mean. It's not all *that* simple, getting an old boat on the water." He considers it a little more. Then he says, "I think we've got all the gear. Help me get her out, Phil, and we'll see what she's like. If she's all right, and the weather suits, I might let you have her tomorrow afternoon. But I'm not promising. Two shillings an hour if I do, and ten shillings minimum, on account of the trouble. Is that all right?"

"That's all right."

"Are you taking this girl out with you?" Sylvia asks.

"Ann? I don't know. I might, if she wants to come."

"It would be fun to make up a four," says Sylvia.

"What, with me?" asks Harold.

"Yes, with *you*, Harold Ericson," says Sylvia, stepping forward and breathing the last three words almost into his face. And for all Harold's dourness and caution, I see the signals flash between them and can tell that the attraction is not a one-way thing. And certainly I'd expect Sylvia—pretty, healthy, full of sparkle—to attract Harold Ericson or anyone else.

"I happen to work here," Harold says. "*I'm* not on holiday." Then he adds, "But my grandpa lets me take a bit of time off during the week. I could go next Wednesday, I daresay."

"Talk to Ann, Philip," Sylvia instructs me, "and see if we can make it a date."

"But you needn't think I'm going in that old tub," says Harold. "If I go, it's the motorboat, and no messing."

"Sailing's more fun," I say.

"*You* don't make a living from boats," says Harold.

I push open the door of the cupboard and step into the tiny hall of the Partingtons' cottage.

"Hello!" I call. "Hello, Ann!"

There isn't any reply. I look into the kitchen, and it's empty. I mutter something to myself, wondering if she's let me down. Then I look round the door of the little sitting room. At first sight it's empty. But she is there, sitting silent and motionless in an armchair in the duskiest corner. I am not quite sure that it isn't a trick of light that makes me think I see her, until she turns her face.

"Ann!" I say again, and walk over.

She gets up, slowly. She is wearing a longish blue-gray dress, drawn in at the waist and with some fullness above

[61]

which partly disguises the flatness of her chest. She is taller, because she is wearing heels. She has reddened her lips. She looks strange to me—not like a young girl dressed beyond her age, but like a young woman whose age is indeterminate. She might be the age she is; she might be twenty; she might be thirty.

She smiles, gravely, and puts out her hand. I take and hold it, wondering for a moment if I'm supposed to put it to my lips. But that seems a bit too much. I let it drop.

"Welcome to the humble home," she says.

"It is a pleasure and a privilege to be here. Especially as an invited guest."

Then I go on, "In plain English, thank you for having me."

She isn't ready yet to give up the game.

"Pray be seated," she says. "I am sorry I cannot offer you an aperitif."

"A what?"

"I can't give you a drink."

"I didn't expect you to. This isn't the Imperial Hotel. Though I must say it looks a bit like it."

The polished table is set for two, and does in fact seem to owe something to borrowings from the Imperial. The place settings are immaculate and there are napkins in silver rings with the I.H. monogram on them. We have soup (she's brought it in a vacuum flask), and cold salmon and salad, and cold apple pie, and coffee (from a flask again). It all feels rather odd: not like being myself at all, but like playing a game of adult life, slightly against my will. Afterwards we sit side by side on the sofa.

I find myself falling into the language of the game.

"I trust this is not improper," I say.

"I fear it is not entirely proper, sir," she says, "since we are unchaperoned, and we are not even engaged to be married."

"Then perhaps I had better take my departure?"

"Oh, no!" she says; and then, "At this stage, that would hardly ameliorate matters."

"Would hardly *what?*"

"Wouldn't make it any better," she says in an everyday voice.

"Let me assure you then, Miss Tarrant, that my intentions are entirely honorable."

"I thank you, sir. Your assurance is accepted."

The artificial dialogue deepens my feeling that none of this is really happening: that it's a game; almost, even, a play. On impulse I half rise from the sofa to drop on a knee in front of her and take her hand.

"Madam," I declare in theatrical tones, "allow me to express my undying devotion!"

"Why, Mr. Martin!" she says. "Is this a proposal of marriage?" And then, striking an attitude in turn, "Oh, sir, this is so sudden! I must have time to consider!"

Then we stop, and look at each other in some bewilderment.

"This is silly, Philip, isn't it?" Ann says. "We shouldn't say such things, even joking."

"No, we shouldn't," I agree with relief. But her eyes are still too expressive for her own good. Getting up from the floor I take her hand for a moment and let it drop. She doesn't excite me physically, but I feel something for her, rather deeply. And along with that I have a slight sense of panic, a fear of stirring emotional depths that would be better not disturbed.

"I'll go and put my ordinary clothes on," Ann says, in common-sense tones. "Then we'll clear the table. Then

[63]

let's go out again, and see if we can walk as far as Craven Head."

But it's a bit too late.

"I . . . think I'd better go," I say.

"Oh, Philip, why? Not because of that nonsense?"

"Well, er . . . I don't know what time everybody'll be back from the outing. I'd like to be there when they arrive."

It's the lamest excuse I could have offered. Ann sees that I simply want to go. She must know she's guessed the reason, but she doesn't try to dissuade me.

"Will you be coming again?" she asks quietly.

"I don't know, Ann. I don't know."

I want to sail. That's what I want to do. I want to sail.

7

"It's all very well for *you*," says my sister Paula.

We're in our own bungalow after supper. Mother is putting Alison to bed. Father has gone round to the Imperial Bar with Mr. Fox. Paula and I are together in the kitchen. She is looking rather sour.

"What do you mean, it's all very well for me?"

"I mean what I say. Off enjoying yourself with Sylvia all day. Coming back for meals, made by somebody else. Never doing a damn thing to help. Of *course* it's all right for you."

Sisterly frankness from Paula is nothing new in my life. Apart from being an outspoken person anyway, Paula has always been a bit jealous of me; and not without cause. She has been a disappointment to Father from the day she was born. If he had had his wish, her name would have been Paul, and she would have been the son he desperately wanted to succeed him in the business. Father was all the more pleased with me, two years later, for being a boy. He was always more pleased with me.

At eighteen, Paula is tallish, dark, and clever. Though some might call her handsome, she is not pretty. She knows all too well that Father does not admire her looks and thinks she isn't a patch on her mother. This hurts. But quite apart from personal questions Paula has a strong sense of justice, which is often affronted.

"Look at you now," she says to me. "Just sitting there like Lord Tomnoddy, reading a magazine and letting others do the work. Who's bathing Alison? Mother. Who's washing these dishes? Me."

"Here, let me do them," I offer belatedly. Paula steps aside to let me get to the sink, but seems all set to continue her remarks. To change the subject, I ask, "What's happening about college?"

Paula is at odds with Father because she's been offered a place at a teachers' training college. He says that most of the cost would fall on him, and he can't afford it.

"No change," Paula tells me. "He says the latest accounts are awful and there's no money to spare."

"Well, he's consistent. That's what he told me about getting a boat."

"A boat!" Paula says, disgusted. "What I'm talking about is my whole future. And what appalls me— positively *appalls* me—is that he's all eagerness for you to go to university when the time comes, and he won't complain about lack of money *then*."

I know this is true, and I understand how she feels. Father is not conscious of favoritism, but he's continually guilty of it. All the same, I feel I have to defend him.

"He doesn't think education's as necessary for girls. They don't have to support a family; they get married."

"And until then a nice little office job will do. *I* know." Paula is fuming.

"And who says *I'll* get married?" she demands.

[66]

"Most people do."

"I'm not most people, I'm me. I mightn't want to marry, or I mightn't get the chance. And if I don't, how does he think I'll feel about the nice little office job by the time I'm fifty?"

"It's no good going on at *me,* Paula. Tell *him.* I'm on your side anyway."

"So's Mother, but even that makes no difference. And what do you mean, *tell* him? I've told him till I'm blue in the face. He just won't listen. Men!"

Paula's voice is rising. I wish Mother would come in and restore peace. But splashing and gurgling sounds from the bathroom next door suggest that Alison's bath is still in progress.

However, there's an interruption. A tap at the kitchen door, and it's Rodney Fox, bringing a book back.

"Men?" he echoes. "What's wrong with men, Paula?"

"Plenty," says Paula. But she won't criticize Father to anybody outside the family, so she reverts to her original subject.

"I was telling Philip," she says, "that he has a lovely time here and lets the women do all the work. Day after day he goes off with Sylvia, heaven knows where, and we go down to the beach with Alison. Why, even you, Rodney, do more than he does to keep Alison entertained."

"I don't mind that," Rodney says. "But I agree with you that Philip is delinquent. In fact, Phil, you and Sylvia are both getting unpopular."

"Sylvia as well? What's *she* done?"

"The same as you. Deserted the gang."

"Does the gang exist any more?"

"Well, it *thinks* it exists. Especially the younger members. Brian and Brenda. They feel neglected, Phil. To tell you the truth, they're not too pleased with me, either, be-

[67]

cause I sit and read and don't join in things. Everybody's fed up with everybody else. We're simmering like a nest of wasps."

"What do you want me to do about it?"

"Come on an expedition to Eastpool on Monday," says Rodney. "The old original six. You and Paula, Sylvia and Brian, Brenda and me."

"I thought you'd grown out of gang outings. What makes you willing?"

"Sheer public spirit," says Rodney. "Some say, 'good old Rodney.' "

"I'll see what Sylvia thinks," I promise.

"Do that," says Rodney. "You could be public-spirited, too, and play tennis or something with Brian. His heart yearns for an opponent."

"I don't know what's come over you, Rodney Fox," says Paula. "Only this spring you were so scathing about everything. Now you're getting so considerate and high-minded. Positively civilized, for a male."

"I'm mellowing in my old age," says Rodney.

"I know what I could do with Brian," I say. "I'm hoping to get my hands on a boat tomorrow afternoon. He might like to come with me then."

My sister Alison comes running in from her bath. She goes to each of us in turn, putting arms round our necks, exchanging kisses and benedictions. Then she gives me a brief account of the trip to Four Mile Beach which Sylvia and I missed. She finishes by telling me about the new striped ice creams on sale at Mrs. Billington's shop at twopence each.

Feeling guilty about my lack of attention to Alison, I dig in my pocket and find twopence.

"Have one on me tomorrow," I tell her.

Alison is delighted and treats me to further kisses. Paula is not delighted at all.

[68]

"How typically masculine," she says when Alison has gone. "You think you can make up for your inadequacies with two pennyworth of striped ice cream. What's more" —and now Paula sounds really annoyed—"it works."

Sunday afternoon.

"I've never sailed before," says Brian, "but I'll try anything once." And then, "What about Sylvia?"

"I'll have a turn later," says Sylvia. "In the meantime I'll just watch. I daresay I shall learn from your mistakes."

We walk together down to Linley Bottom. Sylvia is pleased about this plan, because it will be perfectly natural for her to stay behind with Harold while Brian and I sail. These days Sylvia looks to me like a girl nursing a large and lovely secret. And I suppose that's what she is. She is happy, and the happiness is more than she can contain, so it keeps coming to the surface. In spite of her harebrained scheme I am liking Sylvia these days; she's nice to be with.

Harold grins at us ruefully when we arrive at the slipway.

"Wish I hadn't promised you *Seasprite*," he says. "Took more getting ready than I thought. That sail was a bas—." He glances at Sylvia and modifies his language for a young lady. "A blighter to mend. Anyway, here she is and you can have her."

We take her down to the water on the trolley, and Harold turns her bow to the wind while we get her rigged. It's a slow, stiff, clumsy business, and when the boom swings there are fearsome creaks and groans. She is gaff-rigged with a single large squarish sail of graying canvas, on to which Harold has stitched a big brown patch.

"Homemade and looks it," he says cheerfully. "Anyway, the wind's right for you, and there's no swell to speak of. You'll sail her straight out, and when you come back, if it

[69]

hasn't changed, you'll sail her straight in again. And steer clear of those rocks. And don't be too daft to use the oars if you need to."

I take helm and sheet and we head the boat out to sea. Once under way she doesn't move too badly, though I have trouble at first in getting her to go about. We make a few trial tacks, then beat up past the village and the Imperial Hotel towards North Bay. I am alarmed, looking up from the sea, to note how perilously the Partingtons' cottage is perched on the cliff top. It looks more precarious from here than from the village itself.

We come within sight of the family party on the beach, and there are great wavings and signalings. Brian is already fidgeting to take the helm, and I let him. He is quick to learn new skills, and soon feels confident. He wants to run southwards round Craven Head, but I tell him it will take two hours to get there and five or six to get back, and that shuts him up.

After half an hour or so, during which Brian tries in vain to get the old boat to heel over at a sufficiently exciting angle, he becomes bored.

"I reckon Harold was right about preferring the motorboat," he says.

"It's not like this in a racing dinghy," I tell him.

"All right, I believe you. When you get a racing dinghy I'll come with you again."

"And till then I can keep it, you mean?" I am mildly irritated, because I like boats, even this one. "All right, if you've had enough we'll go in."

Brian wants to steer her in, but I tell him if he isn't interested he needn't bother. He relinquishes the tiller and says, somewhat huffily, that this is about as big a thrill as a child's tricycle. We head back for the Bottom, a good deal sooner than I'd intended. As we go in, the motorboat passes us on its way out. There's no denying that it's going much faster than we are. In it are Harold and Sylvia.

I bring *Seasprite* in without disgrace, though I find that wind and current push her more towards the rocks than I'd anticipated. We get her on the trolley and wheel her up to the slipway, where old Mr. Ericson has taken charge in place of Harold.

I say "old" Mr. Ericson; but actually Harold's grandfather, though his thick stubbly hair is white, has the air of an active middle-aged man. His face is brown but not much lined; his eyes are as blue as Harold's.

"Was that your Harold and our Sylvia?" Brian asks with some interest.

"Aye," says Mr. Ericson. He smiles broadly. "Got to give the lad a chance. He's only young once."

"Hear that, Philip?" says Brian. "Giving Harold a chance with Sylvia." He is entirely without suspicion, and his momentary impatience with me and with *Seasprite* has worn off. "You'll have to watch out, or you'll be losing your girl friend."

"More than one after her, is there?" says Mr. Ericson. "Aye, well, it's not surprising. I can't remember when I've seen a bonnier lass."

He takes out a packet of cigarettes and lights one with a modern-looking lighter, which seems disappointingly unnautical.

"I'll be going, Phil," says Brian. "You'd better wait for Sylvia. I hope she comes back. Maybe you shouldn't count on it."

He is teasing. It wouldn't occur to Brian that Sylvia could be seriously friendly with Harold Ericson.

"Our Harold had better come back," says Mr. Ericson. "And bring the boat. I'm not worried so much about the lass. *She* hasn't cost me anything." He winks.

[71]

"Mr. Ericson," I say when Brian has gone, "you know the Partingtons' cottage?"

"The one that's on the edge now. Next for the drop. Aye."

"How long will it stand?"

"I'm not a prophet. Could be weeks or months. Or days."

"Days?"

"If there's a real downpour it could go. Or a real high sea."

"Might it go in ordinary weather like this?"

"I wouldn't think so," Mr. Ericson says. "But I'd not like to guarantee it. If there's one thing I've learned in a lifetime at Linley, it's that tide and weather take no heed of folk."

"Suppose somebody was in that cottage, might they be in danger?"

"I tell you, I can't answer for things that's bigger than we are. But I've never heard of a person going down the cliff with their house. There's warning signs. A house that's ready to go will crack, and you'd hear it even if you was asleep. And you'd feel it starting to move. Then you'd get out, quick. And it might go in minutes, or it might still be days."

Mr. Ericson looks at me shrewdly.

"But why are you asking, son? Nobody's living in that house now, nor ever will again."

I am cross with myself, and hope I haven't given the game away.

"I know what it is," he says. "You've climbed round the outside and looked in and seen all that furniture. That's what it is, isn't it?"

I nod.

"Well, you take care, lad. You're not a cat. You've only

one life. If I was you I wouldn't risk it climbing around on that cliff. You're a sight more likely to fall than the house is."

"How will the people get their furniture out?" I inquire.

"How would *you* get it out?"

"I don't know. That's why I asked."

"I don't know either. Unless they push it over the cliff and pick it up at the bottom. Which is no way to treat a houseful of furniture. But what are you worrying for? I saw Tom Olsen a few days ago. He's on the rural district council. He told me they'd wrote to the Partingtons twice, to tell them to come and shift their stuff. And they haven't answered. Well, it's their own funeral, isn't it?"

"I'm surprised nobody steals the stuff."

"What, in Linley Bottom?" says Mr. Ericson. He is mildly indignant. "None of *us*'d do it. And visitors don't even know it's there."

He stubs out his cigarette.

"All the same," he says, "it ought to be shifted."

I sit down beside him. There's nothing for me to do except wait for Sylvia. I hope that she and Harold won't be too long, because I've had enough of boats and the Bottom for today.

I find I'm thinking of Ann. In fact she's been just below the surface of my mind all afternoon. I'm wondering if she really ought to be in that cottage so much. What if somebody did come in to steal from it? It would be somebody unpleasant, perhaps very unpleasant.

I am thinking, too, that I'd rather take Ann in the boat than Brian, but that she'd have to be well wrapped up because it gets cold on the water. And I'm thinking that it's not like me to feel so protective.

I must see her again. I can't think what went wrong the

[73]

other day, or whose fault it was, but I must see her. It won't be tomorrow, because we're all going to Eastpool as Rodney suggested. Harold is taking a party out fishing for the day, so Sylvia is free and willing to join the gang. I'll see Ann on Tuesday.

No, I'm not attracted to her. And I'm past the stage of moony first love. But I feel something for Ann, and I wish I had the words to express it.

I wish her well.

And I miss her. It's silly, after so little time, but I miss her.

"Half a mo'," says Mr. Ericson suddenly. "You haven't paid."

I'd forgotten all about that.

"No, I haven't," I admit. "Sorry."

"How long were you out?"

"Just under an hour."

"That'll be two shillings."

"Harold said it would be ten shillings minimum, because of having to get the boat ready."

"He said that, did he?" Mr. Ericson seems half admiring, half shocked. "The lad'll make his fortune if he lives long enough. But it's not my way of working. Either you can have the boat or you can't, and if you can have it you pay the rate and that's that. Two shillings."

8

Monday the seventh of August.

Rodney Fox has borrowed his father's car, and drives us in the clear blue mid-morning along the winding coast road to Eastpool. Summer by summer we've made visits to Eastpool from Linley Bottom. Its pier and promenade and marine gardens are deeply familiar; it stretches back into the shared times of all our childhoods. As the day goes on we feel a return of the gang spirit.

We play a round on the nine-hole miniature golf course. "Pitch and putt" they call it. Brian is intent on success. To him all games are challenges. He takes fewer strokes than anyone else, and is pleased with himself. Paula matches him in determination but not in skill; she does slightly less well and is not quite so pleased. Sylvia and I get by without trying too hard; Rodney does better than we do, but forgets to keep his score so can't prove it. Brenda plays with cheerful incompetence, not caring at all. She takes fifteen strokes at the last hole and nearly a hundred altogether, and is as pleased with herself as Brian.

Then we take a trip on the miniature railway, otherwise patronized only by smallish children, and we wave to pass-ersby and shriek as the train clanks round corners or enters its tunnel. In the afternoon we go to see the open-air concert party, doing its best before rows of mainly empty seats. After that we attempt with little success to win tiny prizes from the greedy machines in the amusement arcade. We find we're all extremely hungry, and buy ourselves a mountainous, rather childish, high tea, consisting mainly of baked beans and scrambled eggs. In the evening we dance with varying degrees of competence in the pier pavilion, out over the sea. We arrive back at Linley rather late, just as the parents are beginning to worry.

My mother is happy to see us all come in together, noisy and animated. She makes us a hot drink.

"It's like old times," she says. "You ought to do it more often."

But to the older ones among us the remark is somehow not encouraging. We know that if we did it too often it wouldn't work.

"We can't stay the same age forever, Mother," says Paula sharply.

It's raining. She stands at the window of the Partington cottage, looking out to sea.

"Ann," I say.

She turns and looks at me silently. I go over to her. She still doesn't say anything, but puts out her arms towards me in an odd, childish way, so that there's nothing I can do but embrace her.

"I thought you wouldn't come again," she says.

"Whatever made you think that?"

[76]

"I don't know. Perhaps it was that—that nonsense the other day. And you didn't *say* you'd ever come again. I thought perhaps you didn't like me as much as I liked you."

"That was a silly thing to think."

"Not really. Anyway, what have you been doing with yourself?" Her tone is light but slightly strained.

"Oh, nothing very exciting. We all went to Eastpool for the day yesterday. You know, the whole gang. I've told you about them. Sylvia and Brian and Rodney and Brenda and Paula and me."

"Was it fun?"

"I suppose so. Quite."

"What did you do?"

"Oh, we played miniature golf, and went to see the concert party, and danced in the pier pavilion. I'm sorry you couldn't come, but . . . ."

I wonder for a moment whether to explain that I couldn't ask her to join us without giving Sylvia's game away. But it's all rather complicated, and I decide I won't attempt to just yet.

"I think I'd be scared, meeting so many people."

"Oh, you wouldn't be scared of *us*. We're all pretty ordinary."

There's a brief silence. Then she says, "I can dance, Philip."

"Do you do it much?"

"Not since . . . Not in the last few months. Would you like to?"

"What, here?"

"Well, we could. There's the phonograph."

I hadn't thought about the phonograph. It's an old windup kind. I wind it and it works. There's a little tin of phonograph needles, and this worries Ann slightly.

[77]

"I haven't actually *used up* anything belonging to the owners before," she says.

"I don't suppose they'd grudge us a few phonograph needles."

"It says sixpence on the tin. I'll put sixpence in."

I am looking through the records. Some are chipped and most are dusty, but there are dance records of last year and the year before. Ballroom, of course: slow foxtrots, quicksteps, waltzes. I put one on. The sound is tinny but bearable.

We dance, not closely. She is light on her feet, so light she hardly seems to be there at all. We pick our way between items of furniture in the sitting room, quickstep out into the tiny hall, on into the kitchen, and back into the sitting room in time to put another record on. We dance three more times. The clockwork of the phonograph is a bit weary, and has difficulty in lasting out to the end of each record, so we finish each time with an involuntary and rather pleasing slowdown. Ann is still a little remote from me, intent, listening for the beat.

After the fourth record I realize that she is breathing rather hard. We are in the kitchen when it stops, and I put her down neatly on a chair at the kitchen table and sit opposite her.

"I'm out of breath," I say.

"Me too."

"It was fun, wasn't it? But I don't think I want to dance any more just now."

"Nor I. . . . It's nearly lunchtime, Philip. Do you have to go back?"

"Not today."

Sylvia and I have gone off with a general blessing on a supposed expedition together. Because we were with the gang yesterday, nobody has grudged us each other's company today. We had a packed lunch between us, but that is in Sylvia's possession. She thought Harold might get hungry.

"I can't give you a proper meal like the other day," Ann says, "but I've got sandwiches and a couple of apples and some biscuits. Will that do?"

"Madam," I say with offended dignity, "I am not accustomed to such humble fare."

She has got her breath back. She laughs, a clear happy laugh.

"Take it or leave it," she says.

"I'll take it."

After lunch it is raining again. Through the window the sea is iron gray. Rain begins to beat on the pane, indicating an east wind.

We sit side by side on the sofa. I find I'm still sleepy after yesterday's active day. I don't exactly doze, but have to struggle a bit to stay awake. Ann is content but thoughtful.

"There was a sail out on the bay on Sunday," she says. "I thought of you."

"Was it a big, square, grubby sail with a brown patch?"

"Yes."

"It *was* me. The boat's called *Seasprite*. I'm hoping to go again tomorrow. Would you like to come? Are you *supposed* to come?"

"Yes, I'd like to. I don't know whether I'm supposed to. I haven't been told I mustn't. It's healthy and out-of-doors, isn't it, so it should be all right. So long as you don't tip me into the water."

"I won't do that. It'd take a genius to capsize that old tub."

"I *want* to go out and do things, Philip. You don't know what it's like, not being able to go and do things,

[79]

until you can't. But it's nice to have somewhere to come back to. . . . Are you happy, Philip?"

"What?" I have almost nodded off, but recover.

"Are you happy?"

"I suppose so. . . . Yes, I am. Yes, Ann."

"I am. I haven't been so happy since—oh, since I was a little girl."

"You're still a little girl."

"Oh, no I'm not."

"Oh, yes you are."

"No. I haven't been a little girl for a long time. I can't really remember what it felt like. But I remember it was happy."

A long pause.

"Would you like to *stay* here, Philip?" she asks.

"What, at Linley Bottom?"

"No, I mean here in this cottage."

"That's a—well, it's not a practical question, is it, Ann? I mean, the cottage won't last long. By next spring it won't be here. And if Rodney's right there'll be a war on."

"There's not much time for anything," she says wistfully. "But suppose there was time, Philip, would you like it?"

I don't understand what she's driving at.

"Well, sort of," I say, "but there isn't, and anyway, it isn't ours."

"I feel as if it was ours," she says. "Don't you feel it, Philip, just a bit? As if it was our own?"

"Yes, I think I do."

"That's nice," she says contentedly.

Another long pause.

"Philip."

"Yes, Ann."

"Nothing, really. I just wanted to say 'Philip.' I like it as a name. Philip Martin. It sounds just right."

"Look, Ann, the sun's coming out. Let's go, shall we, before it starts raining again."

For the third time, we walk on the south cliff. It seems to have become our regular route. We're unlikely here to meet any of the North Bay party. Coming back, Ann leads me along the path that returns to Linley through the churchyard.

We wander among tombstones. They are crowded together, for the churchyard is small, wedged into the hillside. Subsidence has caused the stones to sink and lean all ways, like irregular teeth.

The same few names are repeated again and again. Berg, Billington, Ericson, Olsen, Thorp. Three centuries of all these families; probably more, but the earliest stones have weathered into illegibility. Most of the men whose occupations are given seem to have been master mariners. Apart from deaths at sea, of which there are many, the most usual ages of death are under two and over eighty. Intermarriages among the most common names are frequent, but they seem to have bred a hardy stock.

"I feel a bit sad in churchyards," Ann says.

"Well, that's only natural. Let's go."

"Not just yet. . . . It's because the gravestones only tell you about people dying. Not about people getting born or married."

"You don't need a gravestone for that."

"I know, but, well, it makes you forget the happy things that happen . . . Do you go to church, Philip?"

"We go as a family sometimes. Not often. Do you?"

"No. My parents weren't even married in church. I wonder if it would have made any difference."

"I shouldn't think so."

"I don't know. I think it would seem more permanent, somehow. Would *you* like to be married in church?"

[81]

"I've never thought about it. I don't suppose I'll get married for years and years."

"No, of course not."

We go into the church. Ann puts a handkerchief on her head. The church isn't really old; seventeenth century, maybe. It is squarely built in stone without architectural graces of any kind. Inside, it is bare, bleak, scrubbed; the parish church of a remote, poor parish. Pulpit and pews are of the plainest oak. We wander round. There is not much to see, but the place has a cold, clear beauty that strikes into the mind. Just for a moment I have the feeling that I understand what it is about; then it is lost. As we leave I look for a box to put money in, but there is none. It seems right. This is not a church that asks the passerby for his small change.

Ann takes my arm as we walk towards the churchyard gate and the village beyond. I say something ordinary and she doesn't answer; doesn't seem to hear. I catch and hold her eyes, and her expression is so open and defenseless that I cannot bear it. I look away.

9

My father sits at the breakfast table, eating cornflakes. Beside his plate, still folded, is the morning paper. Paula comes into the room and passes behind him on the way to her seat. Headlines catch her eye, and she picks up the paper and reads two of them aloud: GERMAN PRESS ATTACKS POLAND and MOCK AIR RAIDS OVER BRITAIN.

Father groans.

"*Must* you, Paula?" he asks.

Paula puts the paper down again.

"Sorry," she says. "I realize it's not for me to drag people's heads out of the sand."

"People's *heads* out of the *sand?*" repeats my younger sister Alison, wide-eyed.

"It's a figure of speech, child," says Paula. "We talk about people having their heads in the sand when they won't look at the facts. Which are that it looks as if there's a war coming."

"A war? You mean *fighting?*" asks Alison.

"Yes, fighting."

"Would Philip fight?"

"That's up to him," says Paula.

"I don't suppose it's up to me at all," I say. "If it went on for any length of time I expect I'd have to. I'd be called up."

"You could object," Paula says.

"*I* wouldn't object," declares Alison. "*I'd* fight. At least, I would if there was a children's war. I couldn't fight *men*."

"If there's a war," says Paula, "it won't be wooden swords, I can tell you that. It'll be poison gas and bombing raids. And we'll probably all get killed whether we're fighting or not."

"Don't frighten her, Paula," says Mother. "It doesn't serve any purpose, saying things like that."

"As for heads-in-the-sand," my father adds, "perhaps Paula will tell us what we can *do* about it. And if we can't do anything about it, why should we spoil our holiday by brooding?"

"Oh, it's no use talking to some people," says Paula, disgusted. She shakes cornflakes viciously from the packet.

"Everyone was talking about a war last year," my mother points out, "but it didn't happen. Mr. Chamberlain went to Munich and it was all right."

"All right for how long?" asks Paula. But the question is rhetorical, and nobody tries to answer it.

"Let's look at something more cheerful," my father says. "Such as, SUMMER ON WAY AT LAST." And he reads out part of a news story predicting a spell of fine weather.

And for once it seems the forecast is right. Outside, the sun shines steadily. I call for Sylvia, and we set off for Linley Bottom. As usual, Sylvia leaves me in Middle Row. I ask her to remind Harold that I want to take *Seasprite* out again. By the time I've collected Ann and reached the slipway, Harold and Sylvia have disappeared, apparently to drink tea in Mrs. Thorp's little cafe, round the corner from the Fo'c'sle. But old Mr. Ericson is rigging the boat for us, and it seems no time before we're away.

Ann is wrapped in several woolly garments, which make her seem stouter and more robust than usual, and is wearing slacks. And Mr. Ericson has found a couple of elderly life jackets lying around, and insists that we wear them. Altogether Ann looks rather like an advertisement for car tires.

"Are you nervous?" I ask her.

"Not a bit," she says; and, with a hint of mockery, "I trust you, Philip. I trust you."

"I trust your trust is not misplaced," I say.

Actually there's nothing to be nervous about. The sky is still clear and there's a light offshore wind, enough to move old *Seasprite* along in a leisurely and unalarming manner. And after that brief exchange we don't say a word. Ann sits opposite me. In contrast to active, fidgety Brian, she is at ease, content. She doesn't have to keep moving to balance the boat, for *Seasprite* is broad and stable; and I have nothing to do except hold the tiller. We reach steadily southward towards the northern shore of the headland that culminates in Craven Point.

Dear Stephen, dear Carolyn. I hope you are still with me. I started this narrative with the two of you so much in mind, yet as I have told the story it has drawn me into itself. I halt now because I am at a loss. I do not know how to describe to you a half-

hour in which nothing happens, in which no one speaks, but which counts for so much in two people's lives.

I can tell you that it is a little before noon on Wednesday the ninth of August, 1939; but to say that is to tell you nothing that matters. It is one of those occasions when time seems to disengage itself from clock and calendar and is no longer being ticked away; there is enough of it to last forever. I can tell you that for the next six years this brief spell on Linley Bay, this sense of being in the middle of endless sea and sky and time, is to be my private image of peace, my refuge when life in wartime becomes particularly hellish. But I cannot catch and fix in words the wholeness of such a slight yet rounded experience, any more than I could pin down a bubble.

I can only hint at it; suggest an image or two like the shimmer on the bubble's surface. Images of sun and sky and a squarish gray patched sail overhead. The slap of sea and the mild continual grousing of boom and gaff. The taste of spray, the rough touch of rope and wood. Frail images; I probe them with the pen and they are gone. But for me at least, this is the lasting moment of joy, alive after thirty years; it is the still center of the story.

It is Ann who makes it, of course. We have been wary, have circled and withdrawn and come back; and now, without a word spoken, we accept each other. It is a uniting moment between people of an innocence that in these days must be hard to imagine; a uniting moment between two people who haven't even kissed.

On the north shore of Craven Head there's a worn stone jetty, close by a track that leads up the cliff to the Craven Head Hotel. The track and jetty are older than the hotel, for this was another route of the Linley smugglers. Beside the jetty is a west-facing cove which gets the sun in the afternoon. I. bring *Seasprite* in, and we park ourselves on a rock in this cove and eat our sandwiches. Afterwards we build a large sand castle: no masterpiece of military architecture, I must confess, for it looks as if it had been turned out of an enormous jelly-mould. Ann, serious and intent, collects shells and begins to decorate it.

Then we hear the put-put-put of a motorboat; and it is Harold and Sylvia. They hail us while they are still some distance away, and Sylvia comes bounding across before Harold has even made fast the boat to the jetty.

"You found our place!" she declares accusingly, as if they'd invented it.

But she doesn't mind; not at all. Sylvia is a sociable person, and is as friendly to Ann as if she'd known her for years. Sylvia is also an active person. Harold probably wouldn't mind just sitting for a few minutes, but Sylvia produces a tennis ball and organizes us into a four-cornered throwing game. Ann drops out after a few minutes; she still tires easily; and Harold and I drop out by silent consent a little later. Sylvia bounces her ball against the stone wall of the jetty, first catching it, then finding a flat piece of wood and hitting it racquet-fashion.

"Energy!" I remark to Harold.

"Aye. She's a one," he says; and it's all he says.

Eventually Sylvia's single-handed ball game begins to pall.

"Well, come on, Ericson the Nineteenth!" she cries. "I hope you remembered that swimsuit. You'd better!"

She and Harold are swimsuited under their clothes. Harold groans as Sylvia drags him up from the sand, but livens up when they are in the sea. Soon they are swimming and splashing, laughing and ducking each other and protesting and swimming again. Ann watches, a shade wistfully, hands clasped around knees, as Sylvia runs out of the water and round the two of us, pursued by Harold; then back into the sea again.

Ann turns back to the sand castle and decorates it with more shells, until it is almost covered. I pick up Sylvia's discarded piece of wood and dig a channel from the sea to the castle. Soon it is surrounded by a moat.

After half an hour, even Sylvia is tired. It has become hotter and the wind is dropping, the sky hazing over towards the seaward horizon. Sylvia towels herself vigorously, then lays the towel flat on the sand and herself upon it. When Harold joins her she puts an arm round him and the other, amiably, round me.

"Come and join us," she invites Ann. "Choose your man."

Ann smiles but doesn't say anything. With a hand she scoops out the silting channel from the sea to our sand castle. Sylvia chatters a little but soon falls silent. It gets hotter.

Harold gives a tiny snore. Sylvia withdraws her arm and sits up, smiling. Then she bends over and moves her little finger across the upper part of his body, pretending it's a fly. Harold half wakes up, slaps at it and misses, opens his eyes, sees what Sylvia is up to, pins her hand against himself, and snoozes again. A bit of Ann's sand castle falls into the water.

The tide has come in farther, and will be touching us in a few minutes' time. I say to Ann, "There's not much wind now. We'd better go. The poor old tub'll only just move in this. If it drops any more we'll be rowing home."

Ann says nothing but Harold sits up. He looks towards the graying horizon, then stands and draws his trousers on.

"You should have gone before," he says. "I ought to have noticed."

"Noticed what? Is there going to be a storm?"

"I don't know about that, but it'll blow a bit before long."

"It doesn't feel like it," I say. "It feels stiller than ever."

"Look at the swell."

I look, and can see it rolling in from the North Sea.

"There's something behind that," Harold says. "I've half a mind to drag *Seasprite* right up the beach and take all three of you back in the motorboat. But then we'd have to come another time and pick her up."

He looks at me wryly.

"It's your fault, Phil," he says. "I don't know why I let you have that boat. I wish I hadn't." Then he stirs Sylvia with his toe.

"Job for you," he tells her. "You two lasses can take the motorboat back. I'll sail with Phil in the old wreck."

We are away quickly, with Harold hustling us. We lower *Seasprite*'s sail, and Harold hands the painter to Sylvia in the motorboat. We get a tow for a quarter of an hour, until we're well into the middle of the bay. The girls handle motorboat and tow pretty neatly, and I point this out to Harold, but all he says is, "Not bad for a pair of lasses."

It isn't comfortable out in the bay, because the swell is catching us broadside-on. I hope nobody will be seasick; I don't feel too happy myself. Sea and sky are pewter-colored now.

"Wind's coming," says Harold. "See it moving on the water?" He grins at me. "Nothing to worry about, Phil, but you might get your nice clothes wet."

He yells to Sylvia to drop the tow and scoot for Linley Bottom. The motorboat's put-put speeds up and *Seasprite* is wallowing, well astern in no time. We haul up the sail again, and at once squally gusts start catching it. The wind strengthens but doesn't steady, and poor groaning *Seasprite* is heeling one moment at an angle I never thought she could reach, then tipping sickeningly back to the vertical. I am alternately leaning out and throwing myself back in. I am a bit frightened, but rather more concerned not to be seasick. Harold is grinning.

"Do you like it, Phil?" he inquires at the top of his voice; and goes on, "Of all the stupid ways to get anywhere. . . ."

I suspect that in fact Harold is enjoying himself. I know that I am not. I am wet through; it's raining hard now on the wind, and there's a fair bit of water coming over the gunwale.

Still, the old boat is getting along at quite a speed. The south cliff races past us, then the rocks; and the rocks have come a bit too close for my liking. But Harold knows what he's doing. He yells that he's going about, and we turn three-quarters round through the wind and are running rapidly in towards the Bottom. Now the waves are following us.

"Up centerboard!" Harold shouts, but I'm not quick enough, and it judders on the sand before coming up of its own accord. This brakes us, and a wave piles in over the stern, soaking us both afresh. But the next wave turns over at just the right moment and pushes us sweetly home as if we were riding a surfboard.

In a moment we're dragging the boat up the beach.

The girls are there before us, and old Mr. Ericson is waiting, too.

"Bloody fool," he remarks amiably to Harold. "What if we'd lost our customers? We haven't any to spare these days."

Heads bent, we trudge through slicing rain up the slipway and into Main Street. The girls are as wet as we are.

"I thought we were going to drown," Sylvia says. "A *huge* wave came in."

"I bet it wasn't as big as the one *we* shipped," I say.

"I bet it was. I bet it was *much* bigger."

"Best come into our house and get dry," Mr. Ericson says. "I always keep a fire laid. Only need to put a match to it."

Ann and Sylvia are sent upstairs to change, and come down wearing a wild variety of woolly male garments. Ann's face is pinched and her teeth are chattering. I worry a bit, remembering that she still isn't strong. But we all sit round the kitchen fire and drink very hot, very strong, very sweet tea. Gradually we thaw out. Steam rises from Harold's clothes and mine. We begin to forget the discomfort and feel we've had enormous fun.

After twenty minutes there's a knock on the door. My parents have come looking for me and Sylvia, and somebody has directed them to the Ericsons'. They join the group and drink tea. Later we drive Ann back to the Imperial Hotel.

"I take it she's friendly with young Ericson," my mother says on the way to our bungalow.

"Yes, Mrs. Martin," says Sylvia primly.

"I really don't see why you shouldn't mix with them," my mother says, as if she were answering some objection.

"I should think you don't!" I say indignantly. "We're not in the nineteenth century."

[91]

"There are some who might not quite like it," my mother remarks mildly. I know she's thinking of Sylvia's mother. "But they do seem very nice young people."

Sylvia winks at me. But I don't feel quite so happy about the misunderstanding as she does.

10

"My mother noticed that I was brought back by car to the hotel last night," Ann says.

"Oh?"

"She asked a few questions."

"Yes, I suppose she would."

"She wanted to know if there was a boy involved."

"And what did you say?"

"I had to tell her something about you, Philip. You don't mind, do you? I couldn't *not* have done. She'd realized already that I was spending more time than ever away from the hotel, and wondered what was going on."

"I thought she didn't bother too much."

"She *is* my mother."

"Well, yes, of course."

"Anyway, she'd like to meet you, Philip. She wondered if you could come up to the hotel."

"I suppose so."

"I thought she might have asked you to come for tea on

[93]

her day off or something like that. But actually she's off duty this weekend, and she has to go away. I think she'd like to see you before then." Ann smiles. "To make sure you can be trusted," she adds.

"Very well," I say in the formal manner. "I will endeavor to convince her that my intentions are above reproach."

"It was nice to meet your parents," Ann says.

"Mmm."

"They're nice and sort of *solid,* aren't they?"

"Oh, yes, they're *that* all right."

"I mean in a good way, Philip. As if they'd always be there, whatever happened."

"Yes."

"Do they know *we're* friendly?"

"Well . . ."

"I didn't feel as if they did. I felt as if they thought you and Sylvia were very close."

"I've known Sylvia a long time," I tell her. "Her father was my father's business partner."

"She's nice, isn't she? And I suppose it must seem to your parents that she's very—"

I wait with dread for the word, and it comes.

"Suitable," she finishes.

"I think this weekend we must go and see old Mr. Boland," my father says at breakfast.

Paula groans.

"Oh, no, not that."

"Perhaps we should," says Mother. "It's a whole year since we went."

"It could be the last time we'll ever see him," Father says. "Poor old chap, he's eighty-nine, and he can't go on forever. I talked to Margaret Pilling about it last night, and she agreed we'd have to do something."

Mr. Boland was Mother's uncle. He and the original Mr. Pilling founded the family firm, way back in the eighteen-eighties. My father married into the business, and Sylvia's father grew up in it. Just after World War I Mr. Boland retired and made over his shares to Mother, but our two families continued to visit him at intervals. He lived fifty miles along the coast from Linley, and a trip to see him was a normal feature of the summer holiday. To Mr. Boland himself it was an important event, and he always insisted that his guests should stay overnight.

"Do we *all* have to go?" Paula asks, with an edge to her voice. "I don't want to spend two days visiting old Boland."

"He does rather expect you to, dear," my mother says.

"I don't believe he cares," says Paula. "Philip and I weren't even born when he retired. He doesn't *know* us. All he wants to do is talk about old times, and what do *we* know about old times?"

"Paula has a point, Eileen," my father says to my mother. "I don't really think the old boy would mind. Our children aren't part of his memories, and now they're growing up I wonder if we couldn't leave them."

"I wouldn't like to leave Paula on her own," says Mother.

"Philip could stay, too," Paula suggests. "In fact Philip would *rather* stay. Especially if Sylvia stays. *Wouldn't* you, Philip?"

"I don't mind," I say with careful indifference.

"But who says Sylvia would stay?" asks my father.

"If Sylvia and Brian both stayed behind as well," says Paula, "the rest of you could all get into one car. And just think of all the boredom that'd be saved."

"Well," says Father, "I daresay your mother and I and Mrs. Pilling and Alison would be quite enough for old Mr. B." I can see that he's quite pleased with Paula's

[95]

suggestion. After breakfast he goes round to get Mrs. Pilling's agreement, and he puts his head round the door before going off to play golf.

"Margaret says it's all right, dear," he tells my mother. "So we'll be off on Saturday morning, not too early."

My mother is thoughtful after he's gone.

"Philip," she says, "I know you're very fond of Sylvia."

I murmur something noncommittal.

"But I hope you won't let your feelings run away with you."

I don't say anything.

"You know what I mean, Philip?"

"Yes, Mother."

"Especially when we and Mrs. Pilling are away. I shouldn't like to feel we were putting temptation in your path."

"No, Mother."

"Sylvia's a nice girl, and you must respect her."

Involuntarily I pull a slight face. Mother pats my shoulder.

"Sorry, Phil," she says. "I don't want to be a spoilsport. But I think I still know what it's like to be young. It's so *easy* to be carried away, and you don't know what it might lead to."

"No, Mother."

"Put your arm round me, Phil," says Sylvia as we walk away from the rest of the party. "That's better. We have to keep up appearances."

"I never knew you had such low cunning in you," I say. "And as for luck . . . Honestly, Syl, if you fell in a muckheap you'd come out smelling of roses and violets."

Sylvia laughs. She is full of fizz as usual, living for the moment, eager to get to Linley Bottom and be with Harold.

[96]

"You realize we can't go on getting away with it?" I ask. "Somebody'll tumble to it sooner or later."

"We've managed very well so far."

"I know. But one of these days, by the laws of chance, somebody's going to see you with Harold or me with Ann, or at any rate see that we're not together when they think we are."

"I've got the laws of chance where I want them," Sylvia says. Then, more seriously, "Phil, maybe it can't last, but I don't care. Every day saved is a day gained. I'm so happy it just isn't true."

"There's no future in it, though, is there?"

"Future, future . . . You're just like my mother. 'Think of the future.' That's what *she*'s always saying. But I'm not living in the future, I'm living *now*. And you know what Rodney says about another war coming. If that happens, there's no future for *anybody*."

"All right, all right."

"Of course, if it's bothering you, Phil, we'll have to stop. I ought to have thought of that."

"It's all right."

"Bless you. Don't take your arm away. I like it where it is."

"I've to go to the Imperial Hotel this morning," I tell her. "To meet Ann's mother." I pull a face.

11

The Imperial Hotel is solid, comfortable, upper middle class. It has the air of being built, like Hitler's empire, to last for a thousand years. (And at least it will last longer than Hitler's empire.) Even in 1939 it has tennis courts, a swimming pool, a dance floor. It's not smartly furnished, but everything is clean and well kept and looks as if it had come from the best suppliers. The accents of the guests are not local.

I feel slightly uneasy as I walk through the carpeted lobby. Not that I'm scared by being in the Imperial; I've been here two or three times before. But to know that I'm going to be inspected by Ann's mother makes me feel a bit awkward.

Ann appears from somewhere, wearing a dress. She must have been looking out for me. Together we go across to the reception desk. Her mother is there, making out a bill for a guest.

She is remarkably like Ann: the broad forehead, large

eyes, rather small pointed chin. She's in her late thirties and has kept her looks; for her age she's more attractive than her daughter. She signals us to go through a little gate into the reception area, from the back wall of which opens a tiny office. In it are a lot of pigeonholes, a desk, a typewriter with a half-finished letter in it, and two hard chairs. Mrs. Tarrant says farewell to the guest and brings a stool from the reception desk to join us in the office.

"Well," she says, "so you're Philip." She looks me up and down, taking her time about it. "Yes, you're just like she described you."

Ann's eyes meet mine. She is embarrassed.

"You're in one of the North Bay bungalows, eh?" Mrs. Tarrant says. "Do your family own it?"

"Well, yes."

"I thought they would. They're mostly owned by summer people. Nothing fly-by-night. Well, now, Philip, I don't mind Ann having a friend. It's lonely for her, I'll admit, all those long days, and me working. I can't give her the companionship I'd wish . . . Excuse me."

Somebody is at the counter, making an inquiry. Mrs. Tarrant deals with him. I notice that she has a different accent for the guests.

"You understand, Philip," she says when she returns, "Ann and I are close to each other really, very close, but I'm tied so much by the job. And the manager doesn't think she ought to mix with the guests. . . . Ann, dear, will you just run up and fetch my other handbag? I think it's on the dressing table. If you don't see it there, just look around, it won't be far away."

Ann goes. Mrs. Tarrant leans towards me confidentially.

"She could have a job here, and if you ask me it'd do her good, besides bringing in some money. But the doctor won't hear of it. Simply won't hear of it. Mind you, Philip, I don't want you to make any mistake. She's all right. You know what I mean, don't you? She's all right, perfectly all right, but she has to be careful."

"I understand."

"Actually she's much stronger since she came here. Sea air's good for her. I wouldn't be in this out-of-the-way place myself if it wasn't for that. I've made sacrifices for Ann, Philip. Considerable sacrifices."

"I know. She told me so."

"That's right," Mrs. Tarrant says approvingly. "I'm glad you appreciate the situation, Philip. I think we shall get on very well. Now, I haven't been seeing much of her for some time, and she said she'd been going for walks. I suppose she's been with you?"

"We have been together a bit, these last few days."

"Well, that's all right so long as you don't overtax her strength. I was upset the other night. She was tired out when she got back here, and her clothes all damp."

"I'm sorry about that."

"I gathered you'd been out *boating*. Now that's not right, Philip. I've told her she isn't to go in any more boats. You'll see to that, won't you?"

"I'll take care of her," I promise.

"At least I'm glad she's met your parents. I think it's only right and proper."

I let that pass.

"I have to go away this weekend, Philip. It's my week-end off, and I don't get many of them in this job, as you can imagine. And even *I* need to have some life of my own. It's only reasonable, isn't it? So really I'm quite glad that Ann has you to keep her company. But, Philip—"

"Yes."

[100]

"She's a good girl. And rather young for her age. Remember that, won't you?"

"Yes," I say. It's the second time I've received such an exhortation. It's enough to put ideas into my head. I half smile.

"I mean it," Mrs. Tarrant says sharply. "Oh, here she comes. What, couldn't you find it, dear? I *am* sorry. I must have left it somewhere else. Never mind. Philip and I have had a good talk, haven't we, Philip?"

I nod.

"And now, more guests to be attended to, and letters to finish. No rest for the wage slave. Why don't you two go along to the kitchens and get them to give you a picnic lunch, then go off and enjoy yourselves? And be thankful you're not stuck in a horrid office all day."

"We got on very well," I say as Ann and I walk down the hotel drive.

"She does care about me, you know," Ann says. "She does, really. And so do I about her."

"Of course."

"She doesn't always give the best impression of herself."

"None of us do."

"You didn't find it too awful?"

"It wasn't awful at all."

"At least," Ann says, "we're friends officially now. It's nice to have everything open and aboveboard."

"I have permission, madam, to pay you my attentions," I say. "Though it is requested that I be not too ardent."

"I am sure, sir, that you will always conduct yourself with the utmost propriety. . . . Did she really say that?"

"Yes. Well, she didn't actually use those words. But that's what she meant."

[101]

"Oh, well," says Ann, "I suppose she would. I'm sorry, Philip. I know she needn't. She doesn't *mean* to be insulting."

"I don't feel insulted."

There's a long silence. Then Ann says, "Philip, when you were little, did you play house? You know, being mother and father and going to work and cooking the meals and putting the baby to bed and so on?"

"I think I did, once or twice. With the little girl next door. I wasn't too keen, though. It was rather a sissy game. I'd only do it if I couldn't play with the boys, or with the kind of girls who jumped streams and climbed trees, like Sylvia."

"I used to play it," Ann says, "when I could find a partner, and sometimes by myself. I suppose I was a bit on the delicate side. Though I *could* climb trees."

She muses a while and goes on, "I have a strange feeling about the Partingtons' cottage, Philip. It's been stronger since you came. I've begun to think of the cottage as ours, rather than theirs or just mine. But it's as though it was ours in a kind of game. It's like—well, it's like life, without actually *being* life. Do you know what I mean?"

"Not quite."

"It's more like a home than anything I've had since my father left us."

"Well, it's natural to want a place of your own."

"And yet—oh, there's so little time, Philip. The summer has to end. And I know my mother won't come back to Linley another year. She doesn't really like it. It's not her kind of place."

"Everything seems to be coming to an end this year. But cheer up. Sylvia says we live now, not in the future."

We are silent for some time, both thinking. Then, "Tomorrow," I point out, "my parents will be away, and so will your mother."

"There'll be just us," she says. "Us and our house."

She looks at me gravely.

"Perhaps your mother was right," I say, "to give me that warning."

Ann is startled.

"Oh, no," she says. "I wasn't thinking of that. I mean, well, it *is* only a game of pretend." Her eyes meet mine. "Isn't it?"

12

"Well, they went," Paula says.

"Yes, they went."

"And Mrs. Pilling, too."

"Yes."

"So *you'll* be all right, won't you? A nice uninterrupted weekend. No parents around, no tiresome little sister to get under your feet. Not that you let Alison get under *your* feet anyway. You hardly *see* her except at meal-times."

"Paula, you sound sour."

"I'm not sour. I'm only reminding you how lucky you are. There's nothing sour about that. You've got two whole lovely days to gaze into Sylvia's eyes, or whatever you do when you're together."

"Listen, Paula, you were the one who suggested that the parents should go without us."

"So what?"

"Well, nothing. Only that you talk as if this was something specially arranged for my benefit."

"I sometimes think *everything* in this household is arranged for your benefit."

I sigh. Paula has these times when her frustrations become too much for her. Once a month, usually. She resents *that* as well; and so I suppose would I if I were a girl.

"Anyway, Paula," I say to change the subject, *"you* must be planning something. What are you doing today?"

"That's *my* business."

Paula ponders for a moment, then decides to tell me.

"If you want to know," she says, "I'm going into Eastpool on the train, and I'm going to have a positive *orgy* of driving lessons."

"O-ho!"

Driving lessons are another source of disagreement between my father and Paula. Father is convinced that no girl is capable of handling a car. If Mother drove, he'd think differently; but she doesn't, so he can't see why any woman should.

"Listen, Paula," I say. "Why go into Eastpool and pay for driving lessons? What about Rodney? Mr. Fox lets him use the car, and he's a first-rate driver. He'd teach you."

"I wouldn't ask Rodney."

"Well, I'll ask him for you, if you like."

"No."

"He wouldn't mind, Paula. Rodney always sounds cynical, but he's good-natured. I don't know anyone as good-natured."

"Good-natured!" Paula echoes the phrase with scorn. "You don't even *begin* to understand. I know Rodney's good-natured. I like Rodney, but I'm not going to be dependent on the good nature of some boy. I shall have my lessons and pay for them."

"All right, Paula, all right. It's your own money you're spending."

I remember that Harold and Sylvia are planning to go into Eastpool this afternoon on Harold's motorbike. I hope that Paula won't bump into them, either literally or figuratively. But Eastpool is a big resort, and crowded in August; and it's not really likely that they'll meet.

"What time will you be back?" I ask.

"Not till the last train. I'm going to take myself to the movies."

"I might be late, too."

"That's your business. I'm not interested. You can stop out all night for all I care."

Paula still sounds sour, but from long experience I'm able to detect a relenting note in her voice. And she goes on, "Sorry, little brother. I've been feeling a bit bitchy this morning. If you were a girl you'd understand."

When Paula gets to calling me "little brother," it's almost affectionate. It's also a kind of joke, because I'm slightly taller than she is.

"All right, big sister, forget it."

"Mind you, I've plenty to feel bitchy about."

"I know. You haven't left me in any doubt about that."

"However," she finishes, "have a good time. And listen, Phil, I'm not in the mood to have another row with Father about the driving lessons, so there's no need for you to mention them. You tell no tales and I'll tell no tales. Right?"

"Right."

It's hot, it's hot, it's hot.

The little steam-train chuffs around the rim of the bay: two coaches pushed by a black tank engine.

It's hot, it's hot, it's hot. That's what the train says. Saturday afternoon, the twelfth of August. August weather at last.

Ann and I seem to be the only passengers. When the train arrived from Eastpool in Linley Bottom, no one got off, and no one but us got on.

The world is asleep, and Linley Bottom is empty. All our families and friends have left it today. My parents, Alison, Mrs. Pilling, away this morning on a visit to Mr. Boland. Harold and Sylvia, away to Eastpool just after lunch on the motorbike. The Foxes and Brian Pilling, away by car to watch the summer tennis championships at Four Mile Beach. Paula, away for driving lessons. Ann's mother, away for her weekend off. Now, last to leave and likely to be first back, Ann and I, away on the little train. A tiny outing, just one stop along the line, as far as Craven Head.

It's hot it's hot it's hot. The stuffed upholstery, hot. The grained leather armrests, too hot to touch. Above the seats, the faded sepia photographs of Eastpool. COME TO EASTPOOL FOR HAPPY HOLIDAYS. Holidaymakers in straw hats, or wearing ancient swimsuits with legs halfway down to the knee. Holidaymakers caught by the camera and stuck to a carriage wall for twenty years.

It's hot it's hot it's hot. The windows are fully open. Now and then a whiff of smoke from the engine comes in. The train chuffs uphill, working hard now, climbing towards the ridge that forms the backbone of Craven Head. At last it subsides, thankful and panting, into the station.

A wayside station, empty except for us and the grizzled porter who takes our tickets. A bench, with the station's name in raised letters on its back: C AVEN H AD. Flower beds, climbing roses. A small red brick house with the railway company's initials over the door, and behind it a kitchen garden. The porter has been gardening; his hoe is still in his hand.

The guard waves a green flag; steam hisses volubly; slowly the pistons move; slowly, slowly the driving wheels turn. The train clanks on its way. It's—hot, it's—hot, it's —hot, it's hot, it's hot, it's hot, hot, hot.

Outside the station there's a sign saying TO THE LIGHTHOUSE—1½ MILES. But we don't want to walk for one and a half hot miles. We hesitate. The porter, still holding his hoe, offers to help.

"We just want somewhere to sit," I say. "Somewhere with a view. And later we could do with a meal, before we go back on the six-fifteen train."

"Go along the footpath," the porter says. "It's only a hundred yards to Smugglers' Lookout. And as for a meal, well, you could try the Craven Head Hotel, but they'd charge you plenty. My wife'll make you summat if you like. Boiled eggs and her own bread and scones and a pot of tea—a shilling each. Does that sound fair?"

"Sounds more than fair to me."

"Come back at half past five. That'll give you nice time to catch the train. I won't let it leave without you anyway."

We thank him and go. We don't know whether we find Smugglers' Lookout or not, but anyway we find a flat grassy platform where we can sit side by side and look right across the bay. To seaward a heat haze blurs the horizon. Closer in, there are two or three sails, hardly moving in the still air. Nearer again, and on our left, is Linley Bottom: the south cliff, the rocks, the church, the straggly village, and above it all the Imperial Hotel.

"If we had binoculars," I say, "we'd be able to see the cottage."

"Our cottage," says Ann.

"Now, now. We're not playing a game of house at the moment. It isn't *really* ours."

But I wonder. If the Partingtons have finished with the cottage, isn't it more ours than anyone else's? Just what is ownership? What's pretense and what's reality?

These questions are too hard for an August afternoon. I give them up and think of the next meal instead.

"I shall enjoy the boiled eggs and the scones," I say.

"I shall enjoy the pot of tea. It's still so *hot*."

"By the time we get back to Linley it'll be cooler."

"It's nice," says Ann, "to have somewhere to go back to."

Mid-evening, and the heat has gone. Ann and I are back from Craven Head, full of fresh air and sunshine. I've taken advantage of everybody's absence to rummage in the roof space of the family bungalow and retrieve the gas cylinder and tiny cooker we used before the gas main came to North Bay. I've found an oil lamp, too. The cottage is beginning to seem well equipped.

But Ann is tired. I remember my promises to her mother.

"Maybe it's time I took you to the hotel," I suggest.

"I don't want to go back yet," she says. "I don't want you to leave me, Philip."

"Why?"

"Well . . . I never do want you to leave me."

"You sounded as if there was more to it than that."

"Yes, I suppose there is. You see, if I go back to the bedroom, and my mother isn't there, like she won't be to-night, there's just her empty bed, and I . . . I start wondering about where she is, and imagining things. And then I start thinking about my father, and where *he* is.

And then I don't sleep, and . . . oh, it's horrid, Philip, you couldn't possibly know what it's like."

"I think I can guess."

"You couldn't, because with your parents it's so different."

"Ann," I say, searching for words, "people are only human, and perhaps the way they behave is less awful than you think."

"It's not that I don't think people should be . . . together," she says after a long pause. "I . . . oh, I don't know what I think, Philip. It isn't a thinking thing, it's a feeling thing. I just wish I didn't have to go back to that room tonight."

"Do you?" I ask.

"What do you mean?"

"Well, do you have to go back?"

"I suppose I don't, really. Nobody's going to check up on me."

"Then stay here."

"I don't think I'd like it, being here on my own."

"I'd stay with you."

Unconsciously the conversation has been leading up to this, but I'm still surprised to hear myself say it. And Ann is startled.

"Philip!"

"You sound shocked," I tell her. "Don't worry. I wouldn't do anything I oughtn't to."

"But . . ."

"You said you trusted me, Ann."

"I do. But . . . anyway, can *you* be away and not noticed?"

"Yes, I can."

I remember what Paula said: "You tell no tales and I'll tell no tales." Paula can be awkward, but she keeps her word.

[110]

Ann still looks doubtful.

"We needn't even sleep in the same room," I say.

"Still, being out all night, and alone with each other. It would *seem* awful, wouldn't it?"

"Who would it seem awful to? Nobody would know but us."

She says nothing.

"Would it seem awful to you?" I press her.

"No." At last she smiles. "It would seem right to me. It would *be* right. And I wouldn't want to be in different rooms, I'd want to be with you. But Philip, truly—I don't want to—you know. I'm not ready."

It occurs to me that this is going to be a difficult night. I'm not at all sure that my idea was a good one.

"In spite of the boiled eggs," I say, "I'm hungry. Have we anything to eat?"

"There's a few bits and pieces in the cupboard. And now we have gas we can make ourselves a hot drink."

In gathering dusk we eat and drink, rather slowly. We look out of the window for a while.

"It'd be nicer outside," Ann says. So we go down to the basement and step outside on to the paved area, keeping well away from the edge. Lights are on now. Above is the Imperial Hotel, and there must be a dance tonight, for the sound of music floats faintly down to us. Northward, unexpectedly visible in the far distance, are the lights of Eastpool. Out to sea are more lights, some fixed, some moving.

We drag an old bench from the basement; sit on it; watch and watch. The air is cooling now.

I want to stay here, to stay out for a long time. But Ann shivers. I mustn't keep her in the open.

"Time you were indoors," I tell her.

"Yes, Philip." She's unexpectedly meek. Then, "Oh, I'm so weary."

"Sunshine and sea air, that's what it is. It's healthy."

She takes my hand. We go upstairs into the cottage; then upstairs again, and we're in the main bedroom, which is almost dark.

"I could still go, Ann, if you'd rather. In fact I could still take you back to the hotel. It's not late."

"No."

The room is dusky. We don't want to light the lamp because the window is uncovered.

Slowly, deliberately, Ann takes off her outer clothes and folds them.

"I don't think we should use the Partingtons' sheets," she says. Her voice is shaky. "I'll just get under the quilt and counterpane."

I sit on the edge of the bed. I can hardly see her, but I have the impression that she's shivering.

"Are you cold?" I ask her.

"No. Not really."

For some minutes I sit on the bed beside her.

"You *are* coming, Philip?" she asks at last.

"Yes." In turn I take off my outer clothes. I creep under the quilt and find her. She is awkward in my arms, and still shivering.

"You have cold feet," I say.

"May I warm them on yours?"

"I beg you, madam, treat my feet entirely as your own."

She laughs, nervously.

I am telling myself that Ann does not attract me, never has attracted me, that I feel no physical sensation whatever. But as we grow warm in the cocoon of bedclothes I know it isn't true, it couldn't be true. Yes, it will be a difficult night.

Ann relaxes, doesn't speak. She doesn't know that she is disturbing me, and I cannot tell her. I curse under my

[112]

breath, and she says questioningly, "Mmmm?" I think she's falling asleep.

"Are you comfortable?" I ask her.

"More than I've ever been."

She snuggles closer to me, but I can't bear it and turn onto my back. She is still content, her head on my arm. In a few minutes she's breathing regularly.

I don't feel as if I shall ever sleep. This night has an air of unreality. I lie on my back, and in my mind's eye I see us from far away, here in this cottage at the tip of a tiny promontory, here together in a double bed, chaste. The old-fashioned word echoes in my head. Chaste.

I don't feel as if I shall ever sleep, but I do. And I don't wake until morning. It's nearly seven by my watch, and the sun is shining into the room. Ann is looking at me out of the big eyes, which seem bigger than ever.

"Have you been awake long?" I ask her.

"A while."

"Happy?"

"Philip, yes! You've no idea." She turns to me with surprising warmth, and I turn away for the same reason as before.

"I'm sorry," I say, "but I mustn't get too excited."

I'm not sure at first whether she understands, but eventually she says, "I see. I don't really know about boys, not having any brothers." And after a minute she adds, "Philip, you are *good*."

I don't feel good. I feel at once frustrated and ashamed. I think this is not an episode I'm ever going to be proud of.

"I'll make you a cup of tea," I say.

13

Sitting on the edge of the bed, backs towards each other, we pull on our outer clothes. We are both, I think, a little embarrassed, though heaven knows there is nothing seductive about our utilitarian white cotton underwear. Later, feeling hungry, we stand side by side in the kitchen, sharing whatever remnants of food we can find.

I knock over a cylindrical saltcellar. We watch it rolling slowly along the kitchen table towards the window.

"This place slopes," I remark.

"Mmmm," says Ann. "I noticed that before."

"Yes, but doesn't it slope more than it used to?"

"I don't think so."

"I think it does. And look at the crack that runs down from the corner of that window. That's bigger than it was a few days ago."

"Perhaps it is. Not much, though."

"It'll be all that rain we had the other day. It's shifted

the cliff a bit more. And the high tide with the wind behind it, when we nearly wrecked poor *Seasprite*. That
sucks soil away from under."

"I know," Ann says, unworried.

"I wonder how long it'll be before it goes."

"It'll go when the time comes."

"You're still not frightened?"

"No. Well, you know yourself, Philip, they don't go
without warning. There's always time to get out."

"Even so, it *is* just a bit alarming. And I think of you as
being a nervous kind of person."

She smiles and shakes her head.

"That's not the kind of thing I'm nervous about."

"When you were in the motorboat the other day," I
persist, "and the big wave came in, weren't you frightened
then?"

"Not really." She frowns, trying to sort out her own
feelings. "It was worse when we'd landed and we were
watching you and Harold. That was frightening, seeing it
happen to somebody else."

"You must be noble. I was scared stiff on my own account. I hadn't time to think of other people."

"I'm not noble, Philip. What a funny word to use. I
think it's just that I don't have a lot to cling to. Or didn't.
I mean, when my time's up, all right then, it's up. It
doesn't worry me. But while I'm here I want things to be
right."

"You mean, live for the moment? That's what Sylvia
does. She says we don't know where we'll all be in a year's
time, so we might as well make the most of everything
now."

"No, it's not as simple as that. I don't know how to put
it, Philip. I don't feel I just have to grab what I can before somebody takes it away. I'd like to have a whole life,

[115]

and if I can't it's just too bad, but I'd like what there *is* to be whole. Do you understand?"

"No."

"I'm not sure that I do, either. Anyway, it's changed since last week. I have a different feeling of what my life is. It's not the same for you, it can't be. I know how it is, Philip, I'm not bitter, but in a year or two I'll be the girl you met that summer at Linley Bottom, and in a few years' time you won't even remember there *was* a girl that summer at Linley Bottom."

She is wrong. Even as she says it, I know she is wrong. But on this day, Sunday the thirteenth of August, 1939, I do not know what to say. I say nothing, a stupid, awkward nothing.

Then her head is on my chest and she is weeping. I put my arms round her. In one hand I have a piece of brown bread with a bite taken out of it. Her head is on my chest and she is weeping, weeping.

"I'd like to have years and years," she says, "and be free and strong and go everywhere and do everything, and nothing ever be secret."

I hold her. The brown bread is between my fingers. I would say "Ann, I love you," because I love her, but the words stick and won't come out.

She says, "Philip, I love you."

I hold her more closely. She is flat-chested and I love her. I want to say "I'd do anything for you, Ann," but the words are wedged in my throat like the brown bread in my fingers.

She says, "I'd do anything for you, Philip." She weeps again.

At last, words come to me. From what prompting they come, I do not know. They're silly words, but the best words I have.

"Cheer up," I say. "It's a lovely sunny day and the cliff hasn't fallen yet. So let's enjoy ourselves."

She draws back from me, wipes her eyes, smiles. I eat the unfinished piece of brown bread.

"Yes," she says. "It's a lovely day. I'm happy, Philip. I've never been so happy."

I look at my watch.

"I'm afraid I'll have to show my face at North Bay. They'll be wondering what's happened to me. And with the other parents away, we're all having lunch at the Foxes'."

"I'd better show *my* face at the hotel," Ann says. "Is it an awful mess?"

"You bet it is."

"All right, all right. You've no room to talk. Your own isn't all *that* beautiful. Isn't it time you were shaving?"

"I do shave," I say stiffly. "Every week."

For a moment she is animated, reminding me of Sylvia.

"Be rash and do it this morning," she says. "You've time. And get away after lunch as soon as you can, and come straight back here. And no dilly-dallying."

Then an anxious expression passes over her face.

"We haven't been really wicked, have we, Philip?"

"We haven't been wicked at all."

"I'm glad about that. I wouldn't like to feel we were wicked."

Walking down from the Imperial towards the North Bay bungalows, I come first of all to the Pillings'. Brian is outside, knocking a tennis ball against the wall. He stops as I approach, and looks at me in no very friendly way.

"Up and about already," he says.

"Already? It's nearly twelve o'clock."

"Early enough, considering what time you were out until," says Brian.

I grin, but think it better not to say anything.

"Anyway, what time *were* you out until?" Brian asks. "You spoke as if you knew."

"I know it was plenty late enough. I sat up until after one, waiting for Sylvia. Then I couldn't keep my eyes open any longer. I had to go to bed. She must have come in quietly, she didn't wake me. And she's still fast asleep. I *bet* it was late."

"What are you worrying for, Brian?"

"Listen, Phil, I'm her brother, and she hasn't got a father, and Mother's away. It's up to me to—well, keep an eye on things."

"Guard your sister's honor?" I ask.

Brian is embarrassed, but looks me straight in the eye.

"Well, yes. And I think it's a bit much, keeping her out until all hours."

"Brian, I'm sorry, but there are things I can't tell you at present. But I'll tell you one thing. If you have fears about Sylvia and me, they're unfounded."

Brian is even more embarrassed.

"Sorry, Phil," he mumbles. "I didn't mean *that*. Of course I didn't. It's just that—well, I suppose I was a bit worried when she didn't come in."

I realize that I have managed to make Brian feel himself in the wrong. But my conscience is queasy. What started as a neat and apparently harmless deception seems to have turned into something ugly, hurting other people. And I wonder about Sylvia. Just what am I helping her to do?

"If you want to know anything more," I say, "you'd better ask *her*." That seems fair enough in the circumstances.

"Time she was up," says Brian, "if we're to get to the

Foxes' for lunch. You know how Mrs. F. fusses if people are late."

After Brian, Paula is easy. She is just getting up, and appears in her dressing gown when she hears my footsteps.

"So there you are," she says. "Been out already? Or have you been out all night?"

I can tell from her tone of voice that the second question isn't intended seriously.

"If you'd waited up," I say, "you'd have known."

"And why should *I* wait up for *you?* I'm not your keeper."

I change the subject.

"How did the driving lessons go?"

"Oh, very well. The instructor says I'm nearly ready to take my test. He thinks I'll pass it without any trouble."

"Good."

"That'll surprise Father, won't it, when I come home and wave my license in front of his eyes?"

"It certainly will. Do you think it'll change his views on whether women can drive?"

"I doubt it."

"And will he let you use the car, do you think?"

"I'm damned sure he won't," says Paula. "I'll have to save up for a car of my own. But I'll enjoy showing him that license. And now, little brother, is that really the time? We'd better make ourselves presentable for the Foxes."

"Well, well, so here we are," says Mr. Fox jovially. "All present and correct. Everybody happy?"

He cups a hand to his ear and makes a pretense of listening intently. Nobody answers.

"That wasn't much of a response," Mr. Fox complains.

"Pass me that cold roast beef, Mother." (He means his wife.) "Now, I'm going to say it again. Everybody happy?"

"Yes, thank you, Mr. Fox," says Sylvia politely.

"Oh, we can see *you're* happy, love," says Mr. Fox. "It's written all over you. But look at the rest of them. You wouldn't think they were on their holidays, would you?"

"Father. . . ." says Rodney in a tone of mild protest.

"Anyway, I'm in charge just now," Mr. Fox goes on, "and I'm giving you all your orders. Which are to cheer up and enjoy yourselves while you can. Remember you're a long time dead."

"That's not an encouraging thought at the moment," remarks Rodney.

"Oh, you and your war. There's not going to be one. It was in the paper yesterday, there's not going to be a war. Here's another order. Not a word to be said about wars, on pain of instant banishment without any lunch. Now, Paula, what can I give you? Beef or ham? Here you are, dear. And Brian? What about you?"

"Bit of each, please," says Brian.

"Nice to find that *somebody* still has an appetite. Here you are, Brian. Help yourself to potatoes. Don't be afraid. Take all you want, there's plenty. You don't have to starve yourself like Brenda. Just look at *her* plate. A little bit of meat and tomato, not enough to keep a sparrow alive!"

"I'm slimming," Brenda says.

"Slimming? At your age? Don't be so daft, lass. You'll never get a sweetheart if you're a skinny little thing. Lads like a girl to be a nice armful. Don't they, Sylvia? Eh, Sylvia, don't they? I'll make you blush yet."

"Bernie!" says Mrs. Fox.

"Why, when I was a lad . . ." Mr. Fox begins.

"Bernie!" says Mrs. Fox again, more sharply. "Bernie, please!"

Mr. Fox drops the subject of his youth.

"Now, what shall we give Philip and Sylvia?" he asks. "Lovers' salad, eh?"

Rodney and Brenda groan.

"You know what lovers' salad is?" Mr. Fox goes on. "Lettuce alone." He laughs heartily. "Lettuce alone. 'Let us alone,' see?"

"They've heard it before, Father," says Rodney.

"They'll hear it again, maybe," says Mr. Fox. "Oh, come *on*, all of you. I've been at funerals that were livelier than this."

"Things aren't the same this year, somehow, are they?" says Brenda wistfully.

"Now, Brenda, don't come the wet blanket. We'll be all right when folk get warmed up a bit. How about a glass of cider all round, eh? I reckon you're all old enough now to be allowed a glass of cider."

"Father," says Rodney, "we're not a bunch of kids any more, to be jollied along. People grow up and want to do things their own way."

"And haven't time for the old fogies, eh?" says Mr. Fox. He sounds put out.

"It's not that," Rodney says. "But Brenda's right, it isn't the same as it used to be. It *can't* be the same as it used to be. Life moves on. It's no good clinging to the past."

"If this is what reading clever books and papers brings you to," says Mr. Fox, "I'd rather you were bone from the neck up. I may not be a great thinker, but I've built up a good business and I've enjoyed myself as well. You'd destroy all the fun in life, that's what you'd do, and fill it with all your solemn nonsense."

"Sorry, Father," says Rodney patiently. "I only meant to say we can't expect to be one great big family forever."

"I wish we could do more things together, all the

same," says Brian. "We've hardly done *anything* this year."

"Last year and the year before," says Brenda, "we had an evening picnic. Cooking on the beach over a fire. That was fun. Couldn't we do it again and *everybody* come? Including Sylvia and Philip?"

Sylvia's foot taps my ankle under the table.

"That would be a lovely idea," she says. "Why don't we do it tomorrow night, if it's still fine?"

"There, now," says Mr. Fox with satisfaction, "that's what I like to hear. Something constructive. I reckon we'll all have a good time. But we don't have to wait till tomorrow evening to enjoy ourselves, do we? We can start right here and now. Brian, what about a bit more of everything? Philip, you've had some beef, now try some of the ham. Mother, what about bringing that cider? Here, does everybody know the limerick about the young lady of Hyde who ate some raw apples and died?"

"Yes," says Rodney.

"Well, then, do you all know the one about the young lady of Bude?"

"Bernie!" says Mrs. Fox. "Bernie, please!"

"I thought I'd never get away," I say to Ann.

"I thought you weren't coming. I thought you'd deserted me."

She says this with a laugh, but there's an undertone of relief in her voice.

"Let me assure you, madam, of my undying devotion."

She laughs again.

"You won't leave me, will you, Philip?"

"Of course I won't."

"Not ever?"

"No, not ever."

"But you will. You'll leave Linley in two or three weeks' time."

"Not ever until then," I tell her.

"It's rather a short eternity, isn't it?"

"It may be all the eternity we have."

She changes the subject abruptly.

"This kitchen is a disgrace. I'm going to clean it."

"I shouldn't worry. The Partingtons won't come back now."

"Philip, you're *dreadful*. I don't suppose they *will* come, but I couldn't stand having it like this. There's dust and crumbs and mess everywhere. And just look at the floor."

"Well, *you're* not going down on your knees," I say. "Fair's fair. Let the man of the house have a turn."

I feel I don't mind scrubbing the floor. I am full of energy that has to be released somehow.

I heat water, find a scrubbing brush, and tackle the job aggressively. The rest of the cottage needs only light tidying. We work through it together, feeling a curious satisfaction. It is as if we were taking full possession of it at last, room by room. When we have finished, it is all ours.

But it is hot again, and getting hotter. We finish up standing side by side at the sitting-room window, looking out into burning blue sky and sea.

"You're tired, Ann."

"I'm not!" She is indignant. "Not the tiniest bit!"

"Well, hot, then."

"Yes, I'm hot."

"It would be nice if we—" I begin. I am going to say "could swim," but I remember just in time that she isn't supposed to swim this year.

"Could sit outside," I finish instead.

[123]

"Well, we could sit in the paved area. Where we sat last night. It'll be in the shade now, but I don't mind that, do you?"

Out in the area, Ann sinks thankfully on to the bench we dragged from the basement last night. I still think she is tired. I sit beside her for a few minutes, then I start meditating on the potted plants and hanging baskets in the yard of the end cottage. This rather dim little area could be improved, I feel. I make my way through the row of cottages and come back with an armful of pots. A few of the plants have struggled into flower. An hour's work of collection and arrangement produces some faint resemblance to a garden. I am pleased with myself.

Ann watches sleepily. I reject her offers of help. By the time I finish, her eyes are closed and she is breathing steadily. I make a pot of tea and bring some out to her. She hears the chink of cups, wakes up, puts out a hand. She sips slowly, smiling from time to time, contentedly silent.

I sit on the bench beside her. I am sleepy myself now. I didn't have a totally restful night and have done quite a lot of work. I nod off. When I wake it is half past six. I remind Ann that I've promised to collect Sylvia down at the slipway at seven. Ann sighs.

"The end of a perfect weekend," she says. "Or almost perfect."

"What would have made it *quite* perfect?"

"Oh, just not having to worry about anyone else at all. And feeling it could *last* if we wanted it to. And not having to go off and show our faces to people. . . . Philip, I wish we could be together again tonight."

"Exactly like yesterday?"

"Yes. Don't you?"

I avoid answering the question directly. In a way I do, but in another way I don't.

"My parents will be back tonight," I point out.

"So will my mother. I wonder—"

"You worry about her, don't you?"

"Yes."

"You shouldn't. It's her life. Perhaps what she does in her time off is as important to her as—well, as what we've been doing this weekend is to us."

"But, Philip. Oh, it couldn't be. It *couldn't*."

14

Monday the fourteenth.

"I told my mother I spent most of the weekend with you," Ann says. "I didn't tell her quite everything, of course. Anyway, she doesn't mind. She likes you, Philip. She asked if you'd come and see her again at the hotel some time, and stay for tea."

"Yes, of course."

I am watering the pot plants and hanging baskets that make up our tiny garden. Ann watches me. I tell her, hesitantly, "I promised to be back in good time this afternoon. We're having a picnic supper on the beach."

I can't bring myself to make the next statement: "You're not invited." But when I say no more, she understands well enough.

"It sounds fun, Philip," she says.

"It may not be as much fun as it sounds. Last year it started raining before we'd finished, and the year before that most of the food was burned."

"Oh, what a shame. Still . . ." She doesn't finish the sentence. We are quiet for a while. I finish my watering, and pinch off one or two dead flower heads.

"Philip," she says after a long pause, "your parents are nice, aren't they, and reasonable, and not stuffy?"

"Yes."

"They wouldn't want you *not* to be friendly with me, because of my mother being only a hotel receptionist?"

"No, of course not."

"But you haven't told them about me, have you?"

I don't say anything to that. I can see that she's finding it hard to pluck up courage to continue. At length: "Philip, are you ashamed to tell them?"

"No, I'm not!" It's the first time I have raised my voice to her, and I feel her wince. But she persists.

"I'm happy, Philip, but I'd be even happier if we could be—well, open. If your parents knew about me just the same way as my mother knows about you."

"That's how I'd like it to be. But, Ann, there are other things involved. Other people."

"Sylvia?"

"Yes."

"They think you're fond of Sylvia, don't they?"

"Yes."

"Are you?"

"Do you have to question me like that?"

This time she flinches, and I'm sorry I've snapped at her.

"I am in a way," I say, more mildly. "We've known each other so long, we've a lot in common. Little things, mostly. And knowing we wouldn't let each other down. Yes, I *am* fond of Sylvia. But not the way you mean, or the way they think."

"She likes Harold Ericson, doesn't she?"

[127]

"Yes."

"And *that* seems to be a secret, too."

"Well, Sylvia's mother really *is* stuffy. You've no idea. She'd go up in smoke if she thought her pet lamb was going around with a common boatman."

"It's a bit of a tangle, Philip, isn't it?"

"Yes. It's a hell of a tangle. I don't like it any more than you do. I'll try and find a way out, Ann. I will really."

I am aching to change the subject. And the one I seize on next is a tactless choice. A breath of wind touches my cheek, and I remark without thinking, "Lovely day for a sail."

Just for a moment I glimpse the longing in her face. In spite of those old-fashioned conversations, I know by now how much she wants to go out and do things. After all, it was exploring that brought her to the Partingtons' cottage, not sitting at home. But she speaks calmly, without resentment.

"Would you like to go, Philip? I can't, because I promised I wouldn't. But I don't mind if you do, truly."

I want to say "No, I'll stay with you here," but what I actually say is "Yes." I cannot say anything else. The touch of that wind, the thought of being out on water and away from clogging land, are more than I can resist.

"I won't be terribly long," I tell her.

"Don't hurry. Enjoy yourself. I'll buy some things at Mrs. Billington's shop and make the lunch."

I set out at once, knowing that if I don't go quickly I shall have a tussle with my conscience. She calls after me, softly, as I go up the steps from basement to kitchen, "I still do."

"Do what?"

"Don't you know? Love you."

I would say it to her in return, but the words are still jammed in my throat.

The Bottom is deserted except for Harold and Sylvia. Harold sits on an upturned boat, patiently baiting a line. Sylvia stands two or three feet away from him, one leg forward, her body striking a forceful attitude.

They have been having words. Sylvia's disposition is generally sunny, but she is spirited and can flare with sudden temper at times. I hear her voice as I approach, but can't quite catch what she says. Harold looks glad to see me.

"Here's Phil," he remarks with relief.

Sylvia turns. She is too cross to conceal anything.

"Would you believe it!" she says to me. "He's got his calling-up papers! Got them a week ago! He's joined the Navy!"

"It's not a crime to join the Navy," Harold says. "My dad was in the Navy, one time. *And* my grandpa. And I'd already signed on when you came to Linley, any road."

"Would it have made any difference if I'd been here all the time?" Sylvia asks.

Harold ponders and says "No." Then, as Sylvia opens her mouth, he modifies his remark. "I might have waited a bit," he admits.

"You never *told* me," Sylvia complains. "That's what's so maddening. Here we were, talking about everything under the sun, and you *knew* you'd joined the Navy, you *knew* you'd be getting your papers, then last week you *did* get your papers, and *still* you never said a word!"

"And I wish I'd not said a word now!" Harold is beginning to look out of temper, too. "Listen, miss!"

"What do you mean, 'miss'? You know my name."

[129]

"Listen, Sylvia. There's not much of a living to be made in Linley Bottom, and things aren't getting any better. Men from this village have always joined the Navy. My family and others, when there was more fishermen here, they've all had to do it. And with a war coming and all, now's the time to join up and have a bit of choice while you can."

"When do you go, Harold?" I ask.

"Not till the twenty-eighth."

"That's another two whole weeks, Syl," I point out in reasonable tones. "He'll have been here for the best part of our holidays. And you see Harold's point, don't you? I don't really understand what you have to be cross about, seeing he'd signed on before we arrived."

But Sylvia is not much mollified.

"It isn't *that* I object to," she says. "It's the not telling me. If old Mr. Ericson hadn't let something slip this morning, he wouldn't have told me yet! It just shows how much he cares!"

"It shows nothing of the kind!" retorts Harold. "I didn't want to spoil things, that's all. I know what lasses are."

"Do you?" asks Sylvia bitterly.

Harold shrugs his shoulders in a helpless gesture.

"What can I do for you, Phil?" he asks.

"I wondered if I could have *Seasprite* out again."

"Oh, aye. But we'll have to get her rigged. You should've told me, Phil, and I'd have had her ready for you. Come on, let's do it now."

He turns his back on Sylvia, not sorry to be doing something other than exchange words with her. We get *Seasprite* out and wheel her down to the sea. It doesn't seem to take long this time to get her ready. I'm about to climb aboard when I find that Sylvia is standing beside me.

"Can I come with you, Phil?" she asks.

"Yes, of course."

Harold, impersonally, hands Sylvia aboard. I settle to the helm and we're away. The wind is parallel with the shore and has freshened in the last half hour. A friskier boat than *Seasprite* would be giving us a lively sail.

"Let me have a go, Phil," Sylvia says after a minute or two.

"Think you can manage?"

"I sailed once before, on the reservoir at home. Remember? I think I've got the idea."

"All right." I hand over the helm. "Head into the wind a shade more and keep her close-hauled."

Sylvia is a natural sportswoman, and sailing a boat like *Seasprite* isn't difficult. She soon has everything under control. And, like Brian if not more so, she is eager to get whatever excitement is going. It pleases her most to be hauling hard on the sheet, holding the boat forcibly to its course, and heeling as far as she can get the staid old boat to go—which, fortunately perhaps, is not perilously far. She laughs and grimaces alternately. I can tell that her frustrations are flowing overboard minute by minute; disappearing into the sea.

After an hour she wants to go in. I don't mind, because I feel it's time I got back to Ann. Harold is waiting for us with the trolley, and we wheel the boat back up again. As we stand in the entrance to the Cavern, Sylvia looks him in the eye.

"I hate you, Harold Ericson," she says. "How I hate you!"

Then they are clasped in each other's arms, their bodies pressed together. Harold, unembarrassed, winks at me over Sylvia's shoulder. I don't wink back. Unaccountably, I am not pleased. I sit on the upturned boat formerly occupied by Harold, and wait for them to come out of the clinch.

"See you tonight, Phil," Sylvia says at length, dismissively.

"Don't forget about the beach picnic," I remind her.

"I won't. I'll be in time."

She is in time.

All through a quiet day I've been wondering how to tackle Sylvia and what will be the effect of the latest development. And soon I know.

"Thirteen days to live, Phil," are her first words.

"Oh, rubbish!" I say. "Harold's all right, but it won't be the end of the world when he goes."

But the look in her eye is enough to make me wilt. As we walk back to North Bay I glance sideways at her from time to time, and I can see that nothing less than the Royal Navy or brute parental force is going to detach her from Harold now. I think of her mother, and know that I couldn't possibly give Sylvia away.

The party for the beach picnic is already gathering, at the top of the cliff path near our bungalows. They've decided to start earlier, in order to make the most of the daylight, and are only waiting for us. We stroll towards them, hand in hand. I feel yet again the old uneasiness of conscience. But clearly it isn't affecting Sylvia. To her at present, only one thing matters.

"Well, what have you two been doing today?" my mother asks.

"We've been sailing," Sylvia tells her.

"Did you have a nice time?"

"Lovely. It was just what we felt like doing, wasn't it, Phil?"

[132]

"Yes," I say. "We sailed, and it was fun." It is nice to be truthful now and then.

"I wonder, Philip," Mrs. Pilling says to me, "whether perhaps this evening you could spare the rest of us a little of Sylvia's company."

There's a slight edge to her voice, and I am surprised. I've been so sure that the friendship between Sylvia and myself is approved of that it hasn't occurred to me that anyone might think I'm monopolizing her.

"Of course, Mrs. Pilling," I say dutifully.

We are all sitting on the sand around what remains of the fire. We have had soup from a huge can, and sausages charred on one side and slightly underdone on the other, and piles of bread-and-butter and cake, and smoky coffee with grounds floating in it. It has been a good picnic, as beach picnics go. Now it is nearly dark. Brian, who has appointed himself stoker-in-chief, is still in charge of the fire. My small sister Alison is his grimy-faced assistant, enthusiastic but more a responsibility than a help.

Sylvia gets to her feet and goes across to join the parents. I am left on my own. Not far away, Rodney and Brenda Fox sit side by side. Since getting his university place, Rodney has bought a pipe, and he is smoking it now. Its glow brightens and fades at intervals in the gloom. Brenda, in slacks and a big woolly sweater, sits with her hands clasped round her knees. It occurs to me that they haven't been enjoying this holiday very much. I go over to them.

"Hello, stranger," says Brenda.

"What do you mean, 'stranger'? I see you every day."

"But you don't really look at me."

"I'm scared of being dazzled, that's why."

"You're a witty fellow, Philip," Rodney remarks. "But no longer a sociable one. Preoccupied, I'd say."

"Philip," says Brenda, leaning forward. "Philip, there's something I wanted to ask you."

"Now, Brenda," says Rodney. "Other people's business. Remember."

"I don't care," says Brenda. "I've got to ask him. Philip, there's something funny going on. Every day you disappear with Sylvia, but you don't stay together, do you?"

I say nothing to that. I'm not really surprised, having known from the start that our ruse was bound to be detected sooner or later. All the same, there's a dull thud somewhere in the pit of my stomach.

"We've not been spying on you, Phil. Please don't think that. We wouldn't. But twice we've seen Sylvia with that good-looking boy who keeps the boats, and you weren't around. And another time we saw you coming out of the Imperial Hotel with a girl. And we put two and two together and made four."

"The four being you and Sylvia and the boat boy and the mystery girl," says Rodney. "But maybe we didn't get the sum right."

I am tempted for a moment to try to cover up for a bit longer. But I am sick of deceit, almost physically sick of it.

"You got it right," I admit. For a while I don't say anything more. In spite of the sound of the sea, the crackle of Brian's fire, the squeaks and piping remarks of Alison, the rise and fall of voices from the other group, I feel that I've dropped this admission into a deep silence. Then I ask, "Do any of the parents know?"

"No, I'm sure they don't," says Brenda.

"It's not our business to tell them," Rodney adds.

"But I think Paula suspects something," Brenda tells me. "She's certainly watching you with a beady eye."

"Paula often watches me with a beady eye."

"She's watching you with a *specially* beady eye."

"Thank you for the warning."

"Philip," says Brenda, leaning towards me, "you're doing all this for Sylvia's sake, aren't you?"

"Not really."

"Yes, you are! To give her a clear run with a boy that her mother wouldn't let come within a mile of her. I know that's it."

"You know too much, Brenda."

"Actually, Brenda makes wild guesses," says Rodney. "And sometimes I suppose she has to be right. Well, I for one wish Sylvia luck. Especially at present."

"But who's the other girl?" Brenda asks with interest.

"Oh, just a girl."

"I mean, does she matter? Are you keen on her?"

"Brenda, mind your own business," says Rodney. But Brenda takes a deep breath and continues, "We didn't think you could be, really. Because she's—well, I'm sure she's very nice, but she's not the beauty-queen type, is she? A bit skinny, really."

"For heaven's sake, Bren," Rodney protests. "Be careful. For all you know, you're speaking of the woman he loves."

"Oh, no," I say; and am struck with a sense of my own faithlessness. But now I am seeing Ann through outside eyes. No, she's not the beauty-queen type. Yes, she is a bit skinny.

"You could do better," Brenda says; and now she moves closer to me. "You could do better."

15

Tuesday the fifteenth of August, and it's bright and warm again. Ann stands, as she often does, at the unboarded ground-floor window, looking out to sea. She is wearing a light summer dress and looking pretty; prettier, I think, than when I first met her.

I am consumed with guilt. I can't think why I denied her in front of Brenda last night; I can't think why I allowed Brenda to speak slightingly of her. There must be something twisted in my nature.

"Ann," I say. "Ann." But the words I want to add, all three of them, are once more wedged in my throat.

"Was it a nice picnic?" she asks.

"Quite. The sausages were burned. I don't really think you missed much."

She says no more. But my conscience jabs me yet again. Her life doesn't have a family in it, a gang, communal activities.

"Ann," I say suddenly, not having intended it, "I've got

to tell you all about everything. Then you'll know why I couldn't ask you to come." And I tell her the whole story. In doing so, I realize how much I've wanted to. But I realize also that this is not going to clear my conscience. Part of the burden is rolling off me and on to her.

When I've finished, Ann sits down and says quietly, "I see."

"I'm glad you do."

"Yes, I see." And, after a little while, "Philip, what would have happened if you hadn't met me? What would you have *done* all the time people thought you were with Sylvia?"

"I don't know. I suppose I'd have been all right while the weather was good. I expect I'd have sailed *Seasprite* and gone for walks along the south cliff to Craven Head and so on. And when it was rainy, well, I could have caught the train to Eastpool. There's always plenty to do at Eastpool."

"Would you have liked it?"

"Not much. I'm glad I met you."

"Yes, I suppose it was . . . convenient."

She says this last word in a small voice, barely audible.

"Ann!" I protest.

"It's all right, Philip." Her tone is quite gentle. "I don't mind. I haven't any claim on you. It's just as well to know how things stand."

"But, Ann, listen . . ." Again I want to say "I love you," but still the words are jammed in my throat.

"I told you, Philip, I don't mind."

And now the mixture of guilt and embarrassment in my mind begins to go bad. I find myself saying, "For heaven's sake, don't sound so self-sacrificing. I can't help it, it's a mess, but it's none of my wishing."

"I know it isn't."

[137]

"Well, then, why do you have to ask about the picnic in that wistful tone of voice? I know what you mean. You mean, 'Why couldn't I come to that lovely picnic?'"

"I didn't mean that."

"Oh, yes, you did." My voice is rising. I stand somewhere outside myself and hear it, and I don't like it at all, but it keeps on coming out. "And talking about convenience. Convenience! If you want to know, I met you *before* Sylvia asked me to cover up for her. And if I hadn't met you, she wouldn't have asked me."

"I oughtn't to have said that, Philip. I'm sorry."

But I am not listening to her. It's a kind of destructive madness that's gripping me.

"And you have me here, playing your silly game of house. Scrubbing floors and making meals and gardening. Of all the childish ideas . . ."

She turns her back towards me. I know quite well why this is. It's so that I can't see from her face how much I'm hurting her.

"And as for Saturday night—"

"Philip!"

This time there's terror in her voice, terror about what I might say. I have just enough restraint not to say it.

"The whole affair's been stupid," I tell her instead. "Pointless."

Her voice carefully steady, she says, "I'm sorry if that's how it is. I wish we hadn't started this—this friendship. I've been deceiving myself."

"Division of labor," I say sarcastically. "You deceive yourself and I deceive everybody else."

This time she says nothing. Still with her face turned away from me, she goes back to that window. I know I've punished her for everybody else's faults, including above

[138]

all my own, but it makes no difference. The bad stuff was in my head and had to come out.

"Anyway, we seem to be agreed," I conclude. "We might as well call it off." And, with heavy sarcasm, "Madam, I bid you farewell and leave you in full possession of your property."

She is still silent as I go out. I still don't see her face.

Down at the slipway, old Mr. Ericson sits on the low wall, smoking a cigarette and reading his newspaper. (POLAND "A BLOT ON MAP" SAYS NAZI LEADER.) He looks up and recognizes me.

"They're out in the motorboat," he says. "Harold and the lass. What can I do for you? You want *Seasprite* again?"

"No, thank you. I'm not in the mood."

"All right, lad. I'm not trying to persuade you. Sit down and take it easy. It'll be hot again today."

"Are you expecting to be busy?"

"Nay, I'm never busy these days. Harold's the only customer so far, and he's not paying. I told him yesterday, 'You seem to think I'm here to provide you with summat to take lasses out in. You wait till you're in the Navy, they won't treat you like I do. They'll make you jump to it then,' I said." Mr. Ericson laughs aloud at the memory.

"They'll lick him into shape," he says. "Mind you, Harold'll do all right. He's a good lad and he doesn't lose his head. His dad did well in the Navy. Finished up as a chief petty officer. I wouldn't be surprised if Harold did the same."

"And what if there's a war?"

"If there's a war he'll get promoted all the quicker. Unless he gets promoted off the face of the earth." For a moment Mr. Ericson looks grim, but only for a moment. "Still, it's no use worrying about that. As they used to say in the Great War, if there's a bullet with your number on, you'll get it."

"Maybe the war won't come. But how are you going to manage without Harold anyway?"

"That's no problem, lad. Why do you think he's joined up? There isn't a living for two here, let alone three or four or five, like there'd be if Harold was to get wed. Nay, lad, there's not much doing. I've half retired already. Next summer I might just do a bit of renting, maybe a bit of fishing, but I'm not going to put myself out. I'll have my pension by then."

" 'If Harold was to get wed,' " I repeat. "Is he thinking of getting married?"

"No, no. Course not. Too fond of all the lasses to tie himself to one. But I suppose he'll want to be wed *some* day. Most folks do."

Mr. Ericson gives me a sharp sideways look.

"Mind you, when I say he's fond of the lasses, I don't mean our Harold's always chasing them. No, no, it's *them* that chases *him*. You can't blame the lad."

"I suppose not." I am uneasy again. "When do you think Harold and Sylvia will be back?"

"Oh, not before teatime, I reckon. Not on a day like this. They took their dinners with them."

"I see."

I'm reminded that I too have to eat. I go to Mrs. Thorp's little cafe near the Fo'c'sle and buy a bottle of lemonade and a couple of pork pies. Then I wander up on to the south cliff. I look out over the bay. Sea and sky are blue, blue, blue. There isn't going to be a war. There can't be. Not with the weather like this.

Out on the far horizon, ships pass. Towards Eastpool

there are a few sails to be seen. Close to Linley Bottom there is nothing. No sight or sound of the Ericson motorboat. But Harold and Sylvia must be somewhere around the wide rim of the bay; somewhere, in some tiny cove, together.

When they come in, Harold is cheerful and Sylvia more than cheerful; she is bubbling again, as if yesterday's upset when she heard of Harold's call-up had never happened.

On the way back to the bungalows I tackle her as I'd meant to do yesterday.

"Syl, you know it just can't go on like this."

"Only for twelve more days."

"It can't last twelve days. Rodney and Brenda know. And they think Paula suspects."

"Oh." She is thoughtful now. "Rodney and Brenda won't give the game away, will they?"

"No. And I don't *think* Paula will, though you can't count on it. Paula's unpredictable. There's never any telling which way she'll jump. But in any case, Syl, somebody else will tumble to it soon. Don't you realize it's a miracle the whole thing hasn't crashed round our ears already?"

"Yes, it's a miracle. I believe in miracles."

"Sylvia, I hate to say this, but you know that if they do find us out I shall be in fearful trouble? They'll never forgive *either* of us."

"I do realize, Phil. You don't know how grateful I am. Truly."

"And they'll think the worst about you and Harold."

"They can think what they like. Anyway, they'd be wrong. Harold isn't like that."

"No?"

She looks me in the eye.

"No."

[141]

After a moment she says, "Phil, how could we unwind it all, if we were going to?"

"I suppose we'd just rejoin the gang. Let people think we'd cooled off a bit but were still friends."

"You'd have to stop seeing Ann."

"I think I've stopped seeing her already. We had a bit of a row."

"Oh, I'm sorry about that, Phil. And she did seem so nice."

"It was my fault really," I confess.

"Shouldn't you be trying to make it up, then?"

"I don't know. I don't think so. I feel as if it had all started under a cloud, and the cloud's got bigger and blacker, and there isn't any future in it."

"Oh, cheer up, twin of mine," Sylvia says. "What do you have to think like that for? Sufficient unto the day is the evil thereof. Also the good thereof. Stop worrying and enjoy life. That's what I do."

"Ann's not like you. I think the more I get involved with her, the more I'll make her unhappy in the end. She's well rid of me."

"Philip Martin! I never knew you so inward-looking. I don't know what's come over you. Well, if you don't make it up with Ann you're going to be at a loose end, aren't you? Listen, Phil, you could come with us, we wouldn't mind."

"That'd cramp your style a bit, wouldn't it?"

"It'd be better than not seeing Harold at all. Anyway, it's up to you, Phil. You know how things are. I can't tell you what to do."

"I've decided what to do for the next three days," I tell her. And, suddenly, I have, and it feels right. "I'm going to watch the cricket at Eastpool. Our county against York-shire. A three-day match."

[142]

"Phil! That's like burying yourself alive."

"No, it isn't. You seem to forget. I *like* watching cricket. I've been meaning to for ages. I shall enjoy it."

"You're doing it for me. Or Ann, or somebody. I don't understand. But thank you, Phil. Here, take this." She kisses me on the cheek. "And there isn't even anyone watching. Pure affection, that's what it is. Oh, Phil, I'm *still* so happy. Twelve days to live. Twelve whole lovely days."

16

Eleven thirty in the morning. Still the sun shines. But the outfield is green, not parched. Until the last few days it's been a wet summer. It will take more than a few days' sun to bake the Eastpool cricket-ground brown.

There's a goodish crowd for midweek, several thousand. Out in the middle are the two white-coated umpires. Eleven men in white flannels take up their places in the field. From the pavilion, to a round of applause, come the Yorkshire opening batsmen, Len Hutton and Arthur Mitchell.

Hutton takes guard. The fast bowler for our county paces out his run, stops to make his mark, turns, pauses, polishes the bright red ball against his trouser-leg. Then he is running up to the wicket; his arm goes over, down comes the ball, and Hutton meets it squarely in the middle of the bat and plays it out to mid-off. A fielder trots in, unhurried, and throws the ball to the wicket-keeper, who returns it to the bowler. No run. . . .

And so it goes on. All is quiet, ordered, leisurely. Nobody gets excited. In this long, unhurried day lies a miniature of peace and calmness. The fielders cross and recross, the umpires move in and out from the wicket, the bowlers run silently up to bowl from each end alternately. It's a kind of slow-motion hypnosis, a spacious ballet of white figures on a green ground under a blue sky.

I feel, as I did on the south cliff yesterday, that there cannot be a war. Not this summer, there can't. Even though the word DANZIG jumps out at me from an evening paper, folded as a sun hat to cover the head of a spectator. Even though the memory comes to me unbidden of a drill session with the school training corps, not yet a month ago, when we advanced with fixed bayonets on an enemy squad of stuffed bolsters, swinging from a frame.

"Eh, Leonard, Leonard!" mutters an elderly Yorkshire gentleman sitting next to me, as Len Hutton makes an uncharacteristically rash stroke and is almost caught out.

By lunchtime Mitchell is out for 4, Hutton for 28, Wilf Barber for 25, but there's a promising partnership between Maurice Leyland and Norman Yardley. The old gentleman tells me during the interval about the great days of Yorkshire cricket; about George Hirst and Wilfred Rhodes. Cricket has been his lifelong love. His memories stretch back into the last century—long, sunny memories. Cricket goes on forever.

After lunch, Leyland and Yardley score steadily, taking no chances. And as Yardley drives the spin bowler for a handsome 4, every inch along the ground, I find I am wondering about Ann, wondering where she is, what she is doing, above all what she's feeling. I wonder whether she is in the Partington cottage—*our* cottage—or lying in the grass somewhere along the cliff. Or even languishing in the Imperial Hotel. She may be reading. I know what

[145]

books she reads: Jane Austen, George Eliot, the Brontes. Those are timeless, too.

I know she will be missing me.

Maurice Leyland is out, caught-and-bowled for 64. There's a round of applause as he returns to the pavilion. Yardley looks set for his century.

I know she will be missing me.

Halfway between lunch and tea, cold drinks are taken out to the players. I'm reminded that I am thirsty. I make my way to the refreshment room. And Brian Pilling is there.

He waves to me across a throng of people.

"Phil! Phil! What are *you* doing here?" And when he can get closer, Brian goes on, "Where's Sylvia? Why didn't you tell us you were coming?"

I parry this.

"Why didn't you tell us *you* were coming?"

"Didn't know until the last minute. Mr. Fox and Rodney brought me. They knew I was getting bored at Linley."

Poor Brian. But my God, how young he is. How old I feel in deceit. And how tiresome it is to be put in an awkward spot yet again.

"*Is* Sylvia with you, Phil?" Brian asks. "Best go find her and we'll all join up together. Seems daft, doesn't it, neither of us knowing the others were here?"

Applause floats in through the open doors and windows of the refreshment room.

"Yardley's got his hundred," somebody says.

"Good old Norman!" says Brian. Yardley is his hero: not a professional cricketer but a gifted amateur, which is what Brian himself would like to be.

I know Ann will be missing me.

In the refreshment room the heat is almost unbearable.

"Where *is* Syl?" Brian asks again.

I draw breath, wearily.

"Brian," I say, "she isn't here. There are reasons. Don't tell your mother, will you? Or Mr. Fox? Don't even tell them you've seen me."

Brian stares. He is puzzled, a bit worried. Then he thinks he understands.

"Phil! You and Sylvia have had a row, haven't you?"

I lie without a word, by nodding my head.

"Are you hoping to make it up?"

I nod again.

"Well, I won't say anything if you don't want me to. It all seems a bit odd, though. I thought you and Syl were practically *married*. Anyway, Mr. Fox and Rodney are over there near the sight-screen. Where are you?"

"I'm round the other side."

"You won't bump into us, then. Well, so long, Phil. I don't want to miss any more of Norman Yardley's innings. Hope it all works out for you."

He is gone. I get my bottle of fizzy drink and go back to my seat. A minute or two later, Yardley is out. He's scored 108 runs out of 194 in two and a quarter hours.

"A lovely innings," says the old gentleman appreciatively. "Never gave a chance."

There's more applause as Yardley goes back to the pavilion. The crowd has increased; it may be a record for the ground. Several fielders relax on the grass while waiting for the new batsman.

I haven't had a row with Sylvia. I can't imagine having a row with Sylvia. Sylvia and I understand each other.

But I have had a row with Ann.

I know she will be missing me.

Perhaps she'll be standing at that window where she stands so often, looking out at the sea. Perhaps she'll be sitting out in the tiny paved area. She will be unhappy, and I don't like that. I care about it so much, I must love her. The new batsman arrives at the wicket. I behaved abominably to her yesterday, and I must tell her so. The fielders resume their proper places. The new man takes guard. I hope she'll forgive me. I love her. The bowler begins his run up to the wicket. I love her.

The spectator in front of me is wearing his paper hat the other way round. The word that jumps out now is HITLER.

It is hotter than ever. Not a breath of wind. Unless there's a sudden collapse, Yorkshire look set for a big score. I love her.

> *Stephen and Carolyn, I remember to this day the score at the close of play. Yorkshire made 403; our county replied with 50 for one wicket. But I did not go back on the second or third day, and I never knew who won. Probably it was Yorkshire. It was usually Yorkshire.*

She doesn't answer when I call her name. I look in the two downstairs rooms; no Ann. It doesn't seem as if she's here in the cottage at all. I don't know why I take it into my head to look upstairs, but I do. And she is in the main bedroom, which also has a seaward window, similar to the one in the room below. She stands beside it in the familiar attitude, looking out, her face half turned from me. She knows I am there but she doesn't move.

I go across to her and look into her face, trying to draw her eyes to mine. I think she is resisting at first, still gazing out to sea, but at last her eyes move and she looks at me steadily; unsmiling, silent.

I have rehearsed my opening line.

[148]

"Madam," I say, "I beg to tender my profound apologies."

But as the words come out I know they are all wrong. I wait for the false ring to die away. Then I say, "Ann, I'm sorry."

She doesn't say anything, but when I hold out my arms she steps into them and we stand, embracing each other, for what seems a long time. I am reminded of my parents' embrace in the kitchen, the day I said the dreadful things to my father.

Still we don't speak. Physically I am not stirred, but inside me and all over, from head to feet to fingers, is an emotional pressure that feels more than I can sustain. I haven't felt like this before; I think I shall not feel like this again. I have a sense of commitment that is more than I am ever going to be able to fulfill; an intensity of pain and joy.

Three or four times I've wanted to say to Ann Tarrant that I love her, and the words have stuck in my throat, as if they were too big. Now I can't say them because they are too small. They are trite, almost insulting; the oldest cliché in the book.

Later we eat sandwiches and go out into the sunshine. At the other side of Lower Row, a clothesline stretches across a cottage garden. And it's a lovely, billowing line of washing; white sheets filling with wind like spinnakers; brightly colored towels dancing on air. A joyful, heart-lifting sight.

We stop to look at it, hand in hand.

"And it isn't even wash-day!" I remark.

"Of *course* it's wash-day."

"Nonsense. Wash-day's Monday. Today's Thursday."

"If there's washing hanging out, it's wash-day. That

stands to reason. Happy wash-day, Philip, and many of them. It looks like a celebration, doesn't it?"

"A festival."

"A festival of washing."

"A regatta of washing."

"I want to sail again," she says. "I shall ask the doctor next time I see him. I'm sure I'm fit now. Just look at me. Don't I look healthy?"

"You look wonderful."

Here at last, out in the open air, light-hearted, watching a line of vivid washing as it blows in a cottage garden, I can say it. Cool and clean it comes out without impediment. "I love you," I say.

17

Friday. We sit opposite each other at the kitchen table, sucking through straws at bottles of cherryade. We are a little nervous this morning, a little awkward, wanting to hold each other, not knowing what follows.

Then suddenly we hear footsteps in the next cottage. Quick light clattering ones; slower, more purposeful ones.

The shock is tremendous. We have come here so often and been undisturbed that we don't even mention to each other any longer that we're trespassing. But the knowledge is never far below the surface. We both jump up, and I stride out into the tiny hall.

From the other side of the understair cupboard there are fumblings, as somebody tries to find the way through. Then the door bursts open. Out dashes my small sister Alison, and behind her is Paula.

Alison seizes both of my hands. She is full of excitement.

"Phil! Phil!" she cries. "We *found* you! Paula *said* we

would. We came through a little passage and a whole lot of cupboards!" And then, looking at Ann with interest, "Who's *that?*"

"*That,*" says Paula grimly, "is Philip's friend. Or so I suppose."

Ann stands in the kitchen doorway, white-faced.

"C-come in, Paula," I say. "Into the—er—sitting room."

Alison dances up to Ann.

"What's your name? Are you really Philip's friend? What about Sylvia?"

"What about Sylvia indeed," says Paula. "An interesting question."

"Paula," I say. "Sit down. Let me make you a cup of tea or something."

"Cup of tea? We *are* organized, aren't we?"

"Paula, this is Ann. Ann Tarrant. Ann, you haven't met my sisters. Paula and Alison."

"Ann," says Alison. "Is that really your name? Ann? I like it. I have a friend at school called Ann."

Ann smiles momentarily at Alison, but it's Paula she is watching.

"Well, Paula?" I ask.

"I don't want any cups of tea," Paula says. She looks around her appraisingly. "A nice little place you've got here. A *very* nice little place. Who does it belong to?"

"The Partingtons," I tell her. "That elderly couple from Manchester. Remember?"

"I can't say I do. You have permission to be here, I suppose?"

It's plain from her tone that she is quite sure we haven't.

"Frankly, no," I admit. "We just hope they won't suddenly come back."

Alison now has both of Ann's hands.

"Pick me up, Ann!" she orders.

"No!" I say. "You're too big and heavy to be picked up."

"Well, *you* often pick me up."

"Ann isn't me."

Alison chants:

"There once was a girl and her name was Ann
And she washed her face in the frying-pan."

"Well, Philip Martin," Paula says, "you *are* a dark horse. I thought there was some jiggery-pokery going on, but *this*. . . . An establishment of your own, and not seventeen yet. Congratulations."

"Ann, is it your house?" Alison demands.

"Well, not exactly."

"I can do handstands. Can you?"

"I don't think I can."

"Watch me."

Alison's sturdy legs fly up in the air, then waver back and forth.

"Stop showing off, Alison," says Paula.

Alison returns to the usual way up.

"See?" she says triumphantly. "I can do it." Then, "Is there an upstairs here, Ann?"

"Yes, there's an upstairs."

"Show me it. I want to see it. I want to see everything."

"Show her the upstairs, Ann," I say, "please." And as they disappear hand in hand, I face Paula.

"Why do you have to break in like this, Paula? What do you want?"

"I just wanted to see what you were up to."

Paula smiles. It's not her nicest smile. I am aware once more of her resentment.

"Well, have a good look, Paula, now you're here. As

[153]

Ann says, there's an upstairs. Also a basement. And a kitchen and bathroom, functional in a primitive way if you bring your own water. Any more information you want, you only have to ask."

"There are some people in the world," Paula says, "who always get what they want, regardless of the cost to anyone else. And one of them is my little brother."

The last phrase is not affectionate at all.

"And Alison asked a question," Paula goes on. "I didn't hear any answer to it. What about Sylvia?"

"What about her?"

"Well, to start with, where is she? Not here, I presume?"

"No, she's not here."

"Leaving you with a clear field, I suppose."

"Suppose what you like, Paula."

"Go on, I asked you, where is she?"

"I don't know where she is," I say truthfully, because Sylvia hasn't told me today.

"And who's she with?"

"That's her business."

"*Two* dark horses," Paula says.

"Listen, Paula, we all have our own lives to live. I don't ask *you* questions, do I? I don't mean to be nasty, but honestly, *is* it anything to do with you?"

"Well, yes, actually it is. You have a sister, Phil. Aged seven."

"I know I have. I can hear her chattering away upstairs, nineteen to the dozen."

"She goes on like that all day. Who looks after her?"

"Mother does, I suppose."

"Mother and I do. Today I've got her. Mother would be driven up the wall if she didn't get a break sometimes."

"I seem to have heard this conversation before."

"You heard it last week. I thought you must have forgotten. It certainly didn't make any difference. We still do the dirty work. Call it woman's work if you like, it's the same thing. Cooking, cleaning, child-minding, we do it while you slope off and enjoy yourself. Well, today there's going to be a change, Philip Martin. Woman's work or not, it's your turn to do the child-minding."

"My turn, or else! . . . Is that what you mean?"

"To give you a straight answer: Yes," says Paula.

"O.K., Paula. I suppose it's fair enough, what you say. I hadn't really thought about it."

"There's a lot you haven't thought about. Your friend can have a share, too, can't she? What's her name—Ann? I take it you find her attractive. I must say, she's no Sylvia, is she?"

"Perhaps not."

"Certainly not. Sylvia's a lovely girl, there's no denying it, but *this* one . . ."

"Paula!" I find I'm angry. "There's nothing wrong with Ann. I like her."

"Evidently."

"You think you've got me at a disadvantage, don't you?"

"I *know* I've got you at a disadvantage. It's a nice change. You've always been the one with the advantages."

"It isn't so long," I point out, "since you were talking about not telling tales on either side. What about it now, Paula?"

"I haven't said I'm going to tell any tales."

"You're hinting at it, aren't you?"

Paula ignores this remark.

"Your friend seems to be getting on well with Alison," she says. "I hope it lasts. Alison should be lively company for her, to put it mildly. And Alison's always stimulated by meeting new people. Aren't you all going to have fun?

Mother's having a day's shopping in Eastpool. And I—
well, I think I shall have an interesting day, too."

"What do you mean, Paula?"

"I'm asking the questions today, not you."

Alison comes pell-mell down the stairs, with Ann following.

"It's a lovely little house, Paula," she says. "Just like a
real one. I wish I could stay here a bit."

"You can, dear," Paula says. "Ann has kindly asked you
to lunch."

I open my mouth for a denial, then close it again. Ann
looks surprised, but says, "Stay if you like, Alison."

"There, you see?" says Paula. "Everybody's happy.
Well, I'll be on my way. It's been interesting to meet you,
Ann. *Very* interesting. I'll be able to talk about you to
Philip later, won't I? Good-bye. Good-bye, Alison, dear.
Be good, won't you? Try not to annoy them too
much."

She is gone.

"Ann!" says Alison. "Ann! You look as if you were
going to cry. Are you?"

"No, dear, of course not."

"That's right. You shouldn't cry. You're like a mummy
here, aren't you? Are you a mummy, Ann?"

"No, I'm only a girl."

"You're a big girl, though. You're nearly as big as
Paula. Paula's a *very* big girl. She's grown up, really.
You're not *quite* grown up, are you? You're not too grown
up to play games? I like playing ring o' roses, Ann. Why
don't we all play ring o' roses? This is how you play. You
all hold hands and dance around in a circle, singing
'Ring a ring o' roses. . . .' "

"Take it easy, Alison," I say. "You'll wear Ann out."

"I wear most people out," says Alison with satisfaction.

Actually, Ann and Alison get on together splendidly. Alison is delighted with the cottage. To her, it is like being in an enormous dollhouse. She gets briskly busy with brush and duster; then she insists on watering all my plants; then, standing on a chair, she helps us both prepare our primitive lunch. For seven years old she's pretty capable. She quickly develops a great attachment to Ann, and several times—whether deliberately or by slips of the tongue I'm not sure—addresses her as "Mummy." Ann moves through all this, quiet and patient, kind to Alison but remote, as if anesthetized by the morning's events. She and I have just two minutes to ourselves while Alison disappears into the bathroom. Then she comes to me and we stand clasped together, not saying anything because there isn't time to begin.

After lunch we take Alison down to the beach by the nearest track. She hasn't brought her bucket and spade, but I borrow a full-size spade, a trowel, and plant-pot from the yard where the garden implements are kept. Alison thinks these a great improvement on the conventional equipment. Having made some fifty or sixty sand-pies, we build a sand motorcar, and Alison drives it with much brum-brumming while Ann and I sit in the passenger seats. Then Alison wants to climb on the cliff, and I supervise her with some anxiety. Ann is tired now, and sits on the sand with her back to a rock. We are all thirsty, so Alison and I fetch lemonade from Mrs. Billington's shop.

"I want to paddle now," Alison tells us.

"Good. You can paddle by yourself, can't you?"

"No. I want you to hold my hands. *Both* of you. And swing me over the waves, whee-ee! Roll your trousers up, Philip. Ann, take your sneakers off."

We swing her over the waves, back and forth, and she squeals with delight.

"I'd like to play with you two every day," she says when we put her down.

"I bet you would," I remark.

"Would you like to have me every day?"

"Not on your life."

Alison wonders whether to take offense, but seems to decide that I'm merely being brotherly.

"If you were a daddy and a mummy and I was your child, you'd have me every day."

"And you'd have to behave yourself," I tell her. "Or you'd be spanked."

"Would you and Ann like to have a little girl of your own?"

"I don't know. If she was like you, we'd be tired, wouldn't we?"

"She wouldn't be like me at first. She'd be a baby at first. Would you like to have a baby?"

I look at Ann. Her cheeks are slightly pink.

"I don't think that will arise," I say.

"It might," says Alison seriously. "You never know. People *do* have babies. They wake up one day and find they've got a baby."

At half past five, Alison says quite suddenly that she wants to go back to her real mummy.

I know that the afternoon train from Eastpool will have arrived by now.

"I'll take her," I say to Ann. "And I'm afraid there won't be time to come back here before supper."

"You don't want me to come with you?" Ann asks. "And face the music?"

"There mightn't be any music to face. I can't really imagine Paula giving us away."

"She looked in the mood for it," Ann says. "And even if she didn't deliberately—"

"Well, we'll soon know. I'll see you tomorrow, I hope."

"I hope, too."

"What are you two whispering about?" Alison demands. "I'm ready to be taken back."

"All right, we're going now. Say good-bye to Ann."

Alison hugs and kisses Ann energetically, and almost changes her mind in the process. But I won't stand any nonsense. I drag her away, and we set off along the beach to North Bay. Alison keeps turning to wave to Ann for as long as she is in sight.

18

Ann must have known the game was up. I know it myself, as I enter the family bungalow at North Bay, hand in hand with Alison. It doesn't matter whether Paula tells any tales or not. Alison will talk, and nobody can stop her.

My mother has just arrived back from Eastpool. She is sitting in the kitchen, her shoes already kicked off, and is thanking Brian Pilling for carrying her bag from the station. Father is still away at the golf course with Mr. Fox, and unlikely to return for another hour. Paula stands at the stove, her back towards me, beginning to make the supper. She doesn't turn round.

"So Phil's been looking after you," Mother says to Alison. "I expect you had a nice day, didn't you?"

Alison launches straight into an excited account of all the things that she and I and Ann have done together. Mother at first expresses routine interest and approval, but when Ann's name is mentioned for the sixth time in two minutes she begins to take notice.

"Ann?" she says. "Ann? Is that the girl we gave a lift to in the car a few days ago?"

I nod.

"A nice girl. Mrs. Billington in the shop was telling me about her. Such a pity her health isn't good."

"I love her," Alison declares emphatically. "She and Philip were like a mummy and daddy. They might have a baby."

"They *what?*" My mother jerks upright and the cup rattles into her saucer.

To my horror I feel my whole face flushing crimson.

"It's nonsense," I say. "Nonsense. Nothing like that."

"Well, *anyone* might have a baby," Alison says.

"What's going on?" Mother asks. "Suddenly we hear all this about Ann and a cottage. And what about Sylvia? Where does Sylvia come in?"

"She doesn't," says Paula.

Brian has listened to the conversation, at first with bewilderment, then with an air of understanding.

"Phil," he says in a low voice, "I suppose it's not a secret any more about you and Sylvia falling out?"

"I don't know. Well, actually that wasn't quite—"

"Phil and Sylvia have had a row," Brian announces.

"Oh. Well, nobody mentioned it to *me,*" says Mother. "I must say it all seems a bit odd and confusing."

For a wild moment I wonder if there's still hope of keeping Sylvia's activities out of the discussion. But of course there isn't. Mother and Brian ask almost in the same breath, "Where *is* Sylvia?"

They are looking at me. I say, "I don't know."

But now Paula steps in.

"It's no good, Phil," she says. "I didn't say a word, but the cat's out of the bag for both of you."

"What *do* you mean, Paula?" my mother asks. She is looking worried now.

"I mean," says Paula in a slow, deliberate voice, "that Philip and Sylvia have been going off together day after day, then splitting up and spending the time with other people."

There's a moment's silence while Mother and Brian try to take this in. Then Brian asks in a level tone, "*What* other people?"

"Well, Philip seems to be having this beautiful friendship with Ann."

"And Sylvia?" Brian presses her. "What about Sylvia?"

"Sylvia," says Paula, "has her own light-of-love. And has been with him this afternoon. And I suppose is with him still."

"Who?" Brian demands roughly. "Who?"

"Harold Ericson."

"God!" says Brian. He turns to me: "Philip Martin, I don't know if I can knock your block off. But I'm going to try."

His ferocity is not comic, and I'm not amused. But nervous reaction brings an unintended smile to my face.

"Don't be silly, Brian," I tell him.

"You let my sister carry on with a lout like Harold Ericson!"

"Harold's not a lout. And Sylvia's not a babe in arms. What do you expect me to do about it?"

"I don't expect you to *encourage* it," Brian says. "Covering up for them like that! My God, if Harold was to get her into trouble, I'd—"

"You have a nasty little mind, Brian," I tell him.

"I'm going straight down to the Bottom now. I'm going to sort this out. And I'll see you afterwards, Philip."

[162]

"For heaven's sake, Brian, have a bit of sense. Just *think,* can't you, before you start raising the dust?"

"Oughtn't you to speak *quietly* to Sylvia, Brian?" my mother suggests. "In fact, oughtn't we to wait for her, and *all* have a quiet talk together? I'm so bewildered, I can't really take it all in."

"Perhaps Mrs. Pilling should be told," suggests Paula.

Mother recoils at the thought.

"Oh, poor Margaret! She'd be dreadfully upset!"

"It'd kill my mother," says Brian. "That's why *I'm* going to deal with it."

"Brian!" We are all appealing to him to stop and think. But Brian has a set look on his face. I've seen him like this in a cricket match when going in to bat against a big opposition score.

"I'm the man of the house," he says. "I don't need any help. Least of all *your* kind of help, Philip."

He stalks out. My mother and I look at each other.

"I'll follow him," I say.

Alison has been subdued during all these exchanges, aware of anger and bafflement but only half understanding what it was all about.

"Can I come too?" she demands now.

"No, no, pet," says Paula, plonking Alison on her knee. "It's nothing to do with you. Only a lot of silliness."

I catch Brian up, and try all the way down to the Bottom to reason with him. But he won't listen. Twice he re-rolls his already rolled-up shirtsleeves and clenches his fists.

I hope that he will have to wait at the slipway and will have time to go off the boil. But no, the timing is all too perfect. Harold and Sylvia are just coming up from the

Cavern, arms round each other, laughing. The sight inflames Brian still further. He strides up to them and plants himself in front of Harold.

"Just you take your hands off my sister," he says. "You utter cad!"

I think this is the last time I ever hear the word "cad" used. Even in 1939 it is incredibly old-fashioned. But somehow it sounds more offensive than a ruder modern word would have done.

Harold releases Sylvia. He stares at Brian.

"You *what?*"

"I told you to take your hands off my sister. And keep them off. She's having nothing more to do with you!"

They face each other. They're both in shirtsleeves, and it's hopelessly unequal. Brian is as tall as Harold, but he's still only a boy. Set against Harold's broad shoulders and brawny upper arms, his body looks pathetically slight.

Harold speaks slowly, in a reasonable tone. "That's for her to say, isn't it?"

"Brian," says Sylvia. She is trying to be calm, but her voice has a shaky undertone. "Brian, go away and don't be so silly."

Brian stands his ground.

"You heard," says Harold.

"I'm not afraid of you," Brian tells him.

"All right, so you're not afraid of me."

"And I'm warning you, Harold Ericson. Keep away from her in future."

"Shouldn't you be telling *her* to keep away from *me?*" asks Harold, in the same reasonable tone.

Sylvia looks sharply across at Harold. This last remark is not gallant.

I can see that Brian is still full of aggression. He clenches his fists. But Harold's hands are at his sides, his

[164]

face calm, his manner peaceable. He is not reacting in the way Brian longs for.

"Oh, come away, Syl," Brian says at last, frustrated. "Time we were getting back for supper."

"You needn't worry, lad, anyway," Harold says. "Don't you know I've joined up?"

"He'll be gone in ten days' time," Sylvia tells Brian.

"Less than that," says Harold.

"What do you mean?" The words shoot out instantly from Sylvia.

Harold, who has been unmoved by Brian's attack, at last looks uneasy.

"I was going to tell you," he says. "I'm on my way from here Wednesday morning."

"You mean they've sent for you sooner?" Sylvia exclaims, horrified.

"Not exactly," says Harold. A pause. Then, "I'm going to stay a few days with a pal in Newcastle before I report to the Navy."

"Harold!" I can see that Sylvia, always spirited, is flaring up into a blaze of temper.

"Well, my pal asked me," Harold says apologetically. "I'd have told you in a minute or two, if this lad hadn't come up, fussing."

There's a sharp crack. Sylvia has slapped Harold's face.

Harold steps back, startled. Then he steps forward again, his voice thick with anger.

"I'm not taking that from a lass," he says. Sylvia still faces him, furious. Harold buffets her across the head and sends her staggering back.

"You need to know your place," he tells her.

Sylvia is knocked off balance; perhaps is dizzy. But now Brian springs in to the attack, his fists flailing.

Harold doesn't want to fight Brian. For a few seconds

he lets Brian hit him. But Brian, though slight, is not puny and could damage Harold if this went on. Harold leans forward and grips Brian to him in a bear hug, holding him at too close a range to use his fists effectively.

The area around the slipway is deserted more often than not, but by now five or six people have appeared and are showing interest. Harold pushes Brian forcefully away. Brian nearly falls, recovers, and comes rushing in again. Harold, timing it beautifully, grabs his wrists. Brian can't wrench himself loose, and even in the extreme of anger he wouldn't dream of kicking. Harold holds him for a few seconds, then throws him down flat on his back. Then he turns contemptuously aside.

This time Brian has been shaken, but he picks himself up and seems ready to try again. I put myself in the way.

"It's no use, Brian," I advise him. "Don't make a fool of yourself."

Brian is panting hard, rubbing his back, glaring after the retreating Harold.

"He—hit my sister!" he gasps. "He hit a girl!"

But it is dawning even on Brian that a further assault will do no good. And at least his anger has had a physical release.

"Come on," he says. "It's the end of *that* affair, anyway. Here, Phil, where's Sylvia got to?"

The tiny gathering has dispersed, and Sylvia, too, is out of sight. She can only have gone up the main street. We follow at a run, Brian still breathing hard, and catch up with her. But Sylvia strides ahead, as Brian did a mere twenty minutes ago, and will take no notice of either of us. Her eyes are dry.

Brian addresses her two or three times, gets no response, and at last drops back. He seems unable to sustain his anger against me, but speaks reproachfully.

"You shouldn't have helped, Phil."

"I know I shouldn't," I admit. And it's true. Not for Brian's reasons, perhaps, but it's true.

19

When I get back to the bungalow, my mother is alone in the kitchen. Supper is ready, but won't be served until my father comes in from golf. In the meantime, Paula has taken Alison out to play in the little back garden.

"What happened, Phil?" my mother asks.

I tell her.

"It's a great shame it had to blow up while Alison was in hearing. So unsuitable for a little girl. I hope it won't upset her." And then, after a brief pause, "I think perhaps we shouldn't tell your father, or Mrs. Pilling."

"Mother! I'm sick of hiding things from people. For heaven's sake let's tell everybody everything, and be done with it!"

"No, Philip. It's not that I approve of deceit, but there are times when it's best to keep quiet. Least said, soonest mended."

"Tell Paula that, don't tell me. She's the one who blew the gaff. I hope she's satisfied."

Mother lets that pass. Something else is on her mind.

"Philip," she says, "I was thinking about this girl Ann
. . . What's her other name, by the way?"

"Tarrant."

"That's right, Tarrant. Her mother works at the hotel.
I wonder, Phil, if you quite understand. Did she tell you
she's been in a sanatorium?"

"Yes."

"A *sanatorium*."

"I said yes, she told me."

"Well, you know what *that* might mean?"

"I know she had pleurisy. She's all right now. She has to
be careful for a bit, that's all."

"Well, they *say* she had pleurisy. That's what her
mother told Mrs. Billington at the shop. But I wouldn't
be too sure if I were you, Philip. Nobody likes to talk
about it, naturally, but when a person's been in a sanatorium you can't help thinking about—well, about—"

Mother looks at me meaningfully, but I won't give her
any sign of comprehension, so she has to complete the sentence. She drops her voice so that the last two syllables,
though stressed, are barely audible:

"*T.B.*"

I still stare stonily at her.

"I'm not saying it *is*, mind," my mother says. "But
there's always the possibility."

Something inside me gives a nasty lurch. And yet the
thought is not a new one. In fact it has been present
under every word I've ever spoken to Ann.

"Perhaps," I say with defensive irony, "I should ask her
if she's quite sure she hasn't got it."

My mother fails to detect the sarcastic note.

"Oh, no, Phil, you couldn't do that. It would be a cruel
thing to say. But I do think you'd be wise not to associate

[169]

too closely with her. In fact I really feel it would be kinder to her if you didn't. Because if she's really . . . not in good health, then you don't want to encourage the wrong sort of expectations in her, do you?"

"Of course not. I must be kind and give her the cold shoulder."

This time there's no mistaking my tone of voice.

"Try not to sound bitter, Phil," my mother says. "I'm only asking you to be sensible. Tuberculosis is an infectious disease. It's passed on from one person to another. Young people are specially vulnerable to it. It would be silly to place yourself at risk, now, wouldn't it?"

Something inside me cries out. I could explode with anger; could break things, tear things down. But my mother is so quiet, so earnest. She means no harm. I cannot do violence to her; even verbal violence. All I can bring myself to say is, "I don't want any supper. I'm going."

"Going where?"

"Out."

As I go, Paula and Alison come in.

"My goodness, what a day!" Mother is saying to Paula as I close the door behind me.

An hour later, I am down on the foreshore. I've walked to the Bottom and am now walking back along the beach. It's still light. The tide has turned. Where it's shallow, the sea is brown with particles washed away from East Cliff. This is normal. I look up at the tiny promontory, the little row of cottages on the edge, and as always from this angle it looks alarmingly precarious.

I feel mentally battered. Like this cliff battered by the sea.

In the end it's Mother who has given me the worst

shock. She has exposed one of the reasons why I've been so ready to conceal my friendship with Ann. It's because I knew all along, somewhere below the conscious level of my mind, that this point would be raised. And raised at once.

I believe Ann completely. She would have told me if she'd had tuberculosis. On the other hand, am I quite sure the doctors would have told *her?*

On the other hand again, if she ever did have it, she must be all right now, or they wouldn't have let her out of the sanatorium to go around without warning others, would they?

Above all: I love Ann. I am emotionally committed to her. It doesn't matter what she has, if anything. It can't make any difference. Love isn't conditional, it's absolute.

Nearly dark. Somebody is approaching me along the beach, waving. Because my thoughts have been on her I think at first it's Ann. It's not; it's Paula.

I don't want to see Paula. I can't even be bothered to tell her what I think of her. I am in two minds whether to turn back towards the Bottom. But she'd hurry after me; there could be a silly little scene. I've had enough scenes for today. I stand and wait for her to come up to me.

"Well?" I say. "Satisfied with your day's work?"

"Phil! I'm sorry you're so bitter."

"What do you expect me to be? Delighted?"

"No, of course not. But I didn't mean it to be so horrible for everybody as it turned out to be."

"Paula, it had to be like that. You knew it had to be like that. Don't try to kid me now." My voice is rising; I find after all that I'm indignant; that there's some slight relief to be got from having it out with her. "You gave the game away for Ann and me, and you gave the game away for Sylvia and Harold, and you did it the nastiest way you could. Paula, you're a bitch, and I'll never forgive you."

I push past her and stride on, rather fast, towards North Bay. Paula follows, tries to take my arm, but I shake her off. Then she is half walking, half running alongside me on the wet sand from which the tide has retreated.

"Phil! Do listen to me a minute!"

"Why should I?"

"I've something to say."

"You've said enough for one day. I don't want to hear any more."

"Phil, will you *listen!"*

She runs round to the front of me and plants herself right in my way. The only way to get past would be to push her aside. I could do it, but I don't. I stop, and stare angrily at her through the gloom.

"Phil, try and get this into your head. It wasn't *me* breaking in, it was *reality* breaking in. You couldn't go on playing these silly games, you and Sylvia alike. You *had* to come to earth sooner or later. If it had been later, it might have been worse."

"Oh, I see. It was all done with the highest motives, to save us from ourselves. But you weren't content to *tell* us. You had to do it in such a way that Ann gets nearly frightened out of her wits and Harold gets involved in a fight with Brian. Oh, come off it, Paula, you make me sicker than ever. It was just plain, filthy jealousy. I told you, and I'm telling you again, you're a bitch."

"I understand how you feel, Phil, but—"

"Oh, for heaven's sake, stop butting. You've always been jealous of me. And I expect you're jealous of Sylvia, aren't you, because she's a hundred times better-looking than you are and a hundred times nicer as well. Look, Paula, you've had your nasty little triumph and you've landed us all in the dirt, so for God's sake let it go at that. All you're doing is making it worse."

"Phil, it wasn't all nastiness and jealousy."

"Oh. It wasn't *all* nastiness and jealousy. Well, perhaps that's an admission anyway. Only *some* of it was nastiness and jealousy?"

"I suppose some of it was. I don't always know exactly why I'm doing things, do you?"

"Maybe not, but I don't pretend to be doing people a good turn by stabbing them in the back."

"Phil, I didn't mean it as a stab in the back. A kick in the pants, maybe. And not just on my own account. It was for Mother and—and everybody else. I thought you deserved it."

"Thank you. And Ann? What did *she* deserve? What had *she* done to offend you, or anybody else?"

"I'm sorry about Ann. Truly I am. Listen, Phil, I feel rotten about the whole episode, that's why I'm here. You don't think I *wanted* to have a cozy chat with you just now, do you?"

"It's a bit late to start feeling rotten about it now."

A new thought occurs to me.

"Paula, did you know Ann had been in a sanatorium?"

"I didn't until an hour ago. I do now. I'm sorry about that, too. But, Phil, it adds to what I was saying a few minutes ago. I mean, you couldn't have got seriously involved with Ann, any more than Sylvia could with Harold. It was never *real*, Phil, was it, honestly?"

"How do *you* know what's real? I *am* seriously involved with Ann. I love her."

I'm surprised to hear myself say this, and Paula is obviously startled.

"Of course, you wouldn't know what that means," I add with a last touch of bitterness.

Now we are on our way up the track from North Beach

[173]

to the little cluster of bungalows. Five more minutes and we'll be back with the family.

"I sometimes think nothing seems real this summer," Paula says. "As if it was just before the Flood or something."

"You've been listening to Rodney."

I say it quite calmly. The bitterness has gone. Heaven knows I still have grounds for resentment against Paula, but it's all come out, and I am empty of it now.

"Anyway, little brother, I'm sorry. If I could put the clock back twenty-four hours, I'd have to think again. I don't know if I was right or wrong, I don't really know how it happened. I wish life was simpler. But perhaps when the Flood comes it won't matter."

I say no more. My thoughts and feelings are in such confusion that I can't make any sense of them tonight. What's real, what's serious? I don't know. But surely my commitment to Ann is real and serious.

20

The mournful, hollow sound of the Craven Head fog-horn breaks into my sleep. It's daylight, but still early. I stagger to the window and find we are swathed in a damp, gray-white blanket of mist. I go back to bed, try to sleep again. For a long time I can't; the same old thoughts and feelings are swirling round in my head, punctuated by that monotonous boom. But I doze off at last. I'm awakened by the realization that somebody is sitting on the edge of the bed. Alison.

"It's ten o'clock," she complains, "and nobody's up."

"There's nothing to get up for. Can't you hear the fog-horn? What can we do in this?" ·

"I'm hungry."

"Cut yourself some bread and butter."

"I can't cut bread. You know I'm not allowed to."

"Well, then, have some cornflakes."

"I'm not hungry for cornflakes."

"Do without, then."

"Philip, give me my breakfast and take me to see Ann. I like Ann."

"I can't take you. Anyway, she won't be in the cottage now."

"Oh. I thought she lived there all the time."

"Well, she doesn't." I turn over. But Alison still hovers, and I realize that I'm not going to get to sleep again.

"I'll make you some breakfast," I say, "if you don't fuss."

I get dressed, go into the kitchen, make tea and a pile of toast. Alison and I eat. I take cups of tea to my parents' room. Father is still asleep, but my mother sits up in bed.

"How nice to get a cup of tea," she says; and then, in a low voice, "Philip, I worry about you. I do hope you'll be careful what you do."

I make to move away, but Mother puts a hand on my arm.

"Just for the remaining time we're here," she says, "Don't you think it would be nice if you made a special effort to be friendly to Sylvia?"

"I always have been friendly with Sylvia."

"I mean, you could go about with Sylvia just the way everybody thought you *have* been doing, then Mrs. Pilling wouldn't notice anything, and we could try not to tell her, and we could all continue just as if nothing had ever happened."

"Mother, I am tired of play-acting. T-I-R-E-D, tired."

"I'm not asking you to play-act, Phil. Just to be natural, and perhaps to be specially nice to Sylvia. I'm sure she'd appreciate it. She must be very upset just now."

My father stirs.

"What are you two mumbling about?" he asks; and then, "That's the foghorn sounding."

"Yes," says my mother. "No golf today."

[176]

"We weren't going today," Father says. "Got to spend some time with our families. Though what we'll all do if it's foggy, I've no idea."

He sits up in bed.

"Don't give me time to think about the factory, that's all I ask. Is this cup of tea for me? Thanks, Phil."

I leave the room. I haven't made Paula any tea, but on impulse I push her door open, quietly, to see whether she's awake. She is lying in bed, flat on her back, her eyes wide open and fixed on the ceiling. The movement of the door catches her attention, and she looks across at me.

"Hello, Paula."

"All right," she says, "I'm a bitch."

"I wasn't going to say that."

"I know you weren't. But you said it last night, and it was true. Don't look so forgiving, Philip Martin, I don't like it. I know what I am. I'll try not to be one next time, that's all I can say. With what degree of success I don't know."

"Do you want a cup of tea, Paula?"

"No."

"No, what?" I ask, in the tone of voice we use to get a response of "thank you" from Alison.

"No, I damn well don't."

As I go out, the dismal brazen note of the fog siren sounds louder, seeming to pass right through me. The fog is still thick, but there's just a faint breath of wind to stir it. Now and then the blurred outline of the Imperial Hotel shows itself and disappears again.

The Imperial Hotel. That's where I'm going. But I want to call in at the Foxes' bungalow on the way, to tell Rodney what's happened.

He and Brenda are both up, dressing-gowned, eating

toast and marmalade. Rodney has the newspaper in front of him, and is studying it with distaste. I give him a brief account of Paula's intervention and its results. He doesn't find it as absorbing as I'd expected.

"There's bigger calamities than that on the way," he says. "Listen to this, boy."

Rodney reads me a passage from the paper, about British diplomatic moves in the crisis.

"Pathetic, isn't it?" he says. Then he gives me his views on Adolf Hitler and on the British Prime Minister, Neville Chamberlain, summing them up with a terse indecency that makes Brenda giggle.

"It's not funny, my girl," Rodney tells her. "You'll be laughing on the other side of your face before long."

Then he turns his attention to the question of Sylvia.

"She'll recover," he says. "But I expect it's a case of Rodney to the rescue once more. Good old Rodney. Listen, Phil, I'll borrow the car on Monday if Adolf holds off till then, and we'll all have another day in Eastpool, wallowing in riotous living. After all, it could be our last chance for five years or thereabouts."

"Who's 'all of us'?" I ask.

"The usual, I suppose. Oh, I see what you mean: what about Paula? I think we should take her just the same."

"We don't really know how Brian and Sylvia will react," I say. "Brian wasn't too pleased with things last night. And Sylvia might not *want* to be cheered up."

"Leave it to me. Honest Rodney, the man without any axe to grind. This is my treat, and I shall ask who I like, and that means everyone. It's a time for holding things together, not letting them drift apart. And incidentally, Brenda dear, that applies to your dressing gown, too. Your ample charms are distracting poor Philip."

"I'm quite respectable," Brenda says. "And how do you

know Philip minds? And I'm not all that ample. Just sufficient. Which is more than can be said for some."

Up at the hotel, I find Mrs. Tarrant on duty at the reception desk. She greets me coolly.

"Good morning, Philip. I haven't seen very much of you, after all."

"I suppose not."

"Ann's in her room. Our room, I should say."

"Shall I go up?"

"Oh, no. I'll send somebody for her."

A page is dispatched; it seems that the Imperial doesn't have telephones in the staff rooms. I linger at the desk.

"What a horrid day," Mrs. Tarrant says.

"Dreadful."

"You mustn't take Ann out walking or anything in this. It's enough to get on anybody's chest."

I nod in agreement.

"Of course, if she was well wrapped up, she could go as far as your bungalow. She'd be all right there. It'd do her good, a bit of young company."

I nod again, noncommittally.

"I thought, being friendly with you, she might have mixed with your family and the young people more," Mrs. Tarrant says. "But it doesn't seem to have happened."

"No." And then, because the question is eating me, I ask, "Mrs. Tarrant, is she getting better? I mean, is she getting better *quickly?*"

Mrs. Tarrant looks sharply at me.

"So people have been talking, have they? What do they say?"

"I don't know."

"It's wicked, the way it follows you around. I've seen

[179]

folk look at me as if I'd done something awful. Well, I can guess what they're saying. And let me tell you, young man, in plain words, my girl hasn't got T.B. and never did have. Pleurisy, that's what it was, and by the end of this summer she'll be as right as rain."

The page boy scoots past, calling "She's coming."

"Do you believe me?" Mrs. Tarrant demands.

"Yes, of course."

"Then if anybody says any more, you just tell them that."

Ann appears. She's wearing a white woollen cardigan over a dress. She looks pale and serious. Not a patch on Sylvia. No ample charms like Brenda's. Maybe not, but I love her.

"I thought," Mrs. Tarrant says to Ann, "that on a day like this Philip might have taken you down to North Bay. A bit of young company would do you good, I told him."

I wonder for a moment whether I dare take Ann down to the bungalows. But the situation is awkward and could be explosive. It would be silly to plunge her into that.

So I keep silent, and Ann comes to my rescue by saying calmly, "I oughtn't to go out in this anyway. Come along, Philip, we'll look for somewhere to sit."

We find a settee in a corner of the residents' lounge. The room is filling up, because nobody wants to go out in the fog. It's a small rustling forest of newspapers, with the headlines that we're all used to but that are now multiplying ominously: DEEPENING CRISIS and NEW NAZI THREAT, and the endlessly repeated words HITLER, DANZIG, POLAND.

I begin telling Ann what has happened since Alison and I left her on the beach. She listens quietly, her fingers drumming on the arm of the settee.

Near us, four people start a game of bridge. My narrative is punctuated by their bids. "Two hearts," "Two

[180]

spades," "Three no trumps." Ann says "Poor Sylvia," almost inaudibly. Half a dozen new arrivals gather in the doorway, looking for somewhere to sit.

Ann is uneasy. "I think we'd better go, Philip," she says. "The room's full. If the manager saw us, he'd tell us not to take up seats needed for the residents."

Down in the basement, opening out of the kitchens, there's a staff room. A contrast with the carpeted, overstuffed lounge. Bare floor, bare chairs, bare tables. A fair amount of noise, for the off-duty staff are as much confined by fog as the residents are. Ann gets two mugs of tea for us from the kitchen: hot, sweet, stewed. We sit opposite each other at a table, sipping. Some of the staff greet Ann, but nobody actually talks to us. I try to resume my story, but it's difficult because of the noise. There's no peace or comfort for us here.

We go back to the lobby. Ann has a brief word with her mother. She comes away smiling ruefully.

"I suggested we should go to my room. But Mother didn't think that would be quite nice."

"We've nowhere to go," I say. "Refugees." But newsreel pictures of real refugees come to my mind, and I drop the comparison rapidly.

We sit side by side on a leather bench in the lobby for quite a while. We are not directly under the eye of Mrs. Tarrant, but are very much aware of her presence at the reception desk in the corner. We don't feel we can even hold hands. An elderly couple opposite us stare blankly at nothing, taking no notice even of each other. Nobody else is sitting in the lobby, but occasionally people cross it, and now and then the main door opens, letting in a cold draught, a wisp or two of fog, and the sound of the siren.

I had so much to tell Ann, but somehow, now I have given her the bare outline of the story, there seems nothing else to say.

[181]

I am empty of words. I would love and cherish her forever, but even the words to say that will not come. All that will arrive on my lips is, "I think I'd better be going."

"There isn't anywhere for us, is there?" Ann says. "It's not like the cottage, our own place." And, after a minute, hesitantly, "Will you go to the cottage again, Philip? *Can* you? Or is *everything* finished?"

"No, everything's not finished. But my parents are taking us all out tomorrow if the fog clears, and on Monday I'll have to go to Eastpool again with the gang. What about Tuesday?"

"Yes, Tuesday. It's Mother's day off again by then. I expect she'll go away."

"I'll see you Tuesday, then."

"Yes." She murmurs something, half aside.

"What did you say, Ann?"

"Nothing, Philip."

But the half-heard words sort themselves out in my head. She's said it's a long time till Tuesday.

Time, time, time. I want to say that one day I'll annihilate it and be with her for always. But what I actually say is, "All right, then. I'll be on my way."

I go over to the desk and say "Good-bye" to Mrs. Tarrant. She bids me a chilly farewell. I give Ann a small wave as I pass her on the way out, and she gives me a very small smile. Then I am out in the fog. I am glad to be away from the Imperial Hotel. I am glad to be away from Mrs. Tarrant. This morning I am glad to be away from Ann, too. It's been as if I were seeing her through glass; worse than not seeing her at all.

The fog crawls clammily into my throat. I cough. The mournful sound of the siren floats across from Craven Head. Again and again. Again and again and again.

21

Monday the twenty-first of August. Cloudy, with a suspicion of rain—or it might be spray—carried on the
wind.

Rodney drives us into Eastpool. I am liking him more
today than I've ever done. He is lively, at his best, rallying
round Sylvia. She sits beside him in the front of the car.
Brian, Brenda, and I are in the back. Paula has not come
after all; she seems for the moment to be sunk in self-dis-
gust. Sylvia is subdued at first, but the rest of us chatter
and tease each other busily. By the time we've parked the
car in Eastpool, I feel we have almost returned to shape as
a cheerful holiday party.

Rodney buys an early edition of the evening paper,
glances at the front page, crumples it without comment,
and drops it into the nearest litter-bin. Then he goes on
joking with Sylvia.

The number of things you can do in Eastpool isn't un-
limited. Our program is much the same as when we came

before, but by mid-afternoon the suspicion of rain has become fact; it is blowing in great wet gusts from the sea. The open-air performance of the concert party is called off. We go to the cinema instead and see a new Fred Astaire–Ginger Rogers film. As we come out, Rodney drops behind, buys another paper, and again barely glances at it.

Towards dusk the rain eases, and for a time the sky clears. We walk arm in arm, all five abreast, to the end of the pier, and lean over the railings, far out above the incoming tide. Brenda is beside me, pressing against me, shoulder, hip, and leg. There's something about a pier— that frail extension of land over sea—that always gives a feeling of strangeness. To landward, where the sun sets, the sky is a pale, wet gold; almost like an upturned beach. I don't quite know where we are.

We find we are singing. First a couple of songs from the new film: uncertainly, because most of us haven't heard them before, and are not sure of words or tune. Then, unaccountably, it's songs from the Great War that we're singing: "Tipperary" and "There's a long, long trail a-winding." Among the five of us, only Sylvia can really sing: a clear, unself-conscious soprano from which, after a while, the rest of us let our voices drop away.

From "There's a long, long trail" we move on to "All through the night" and then to the hymn "Eternal Father, strong to save, Whose arm doth bind the restless wave." Rodney, who doesn't believe in God, sings as seriously as anyone. But after the first verse only Sylvia knows the words. She knows them because this hymn is a favorite of the rector, back at our city church; she has sung it again and again through the years. "And ever let there rise to Thee, Glad hymns of praise from land and sea," she finishes; and then she's sobbing helplessly and Rodney is comforting her; and then the rain is pouring again, driv-

[184]

ing us off the pier and into the shiny, colored-light-reflecting streets of the resort.

Sylvia is all right now. The tears have been a kind of rainstorm, washing her troubles away. Her voice rings out, clear and happy. We buy and eat fish and chips, at the little shop where we bought them on the way to Linley, three weeks ago. Then we go into a little back-street pub where they don't worry too much about whether people are of age. Rodney and I have a glass of beer each, and the others soft drinks. There's singing again: not started by us, but much improved by Sylvia's voice. The old Saturday night pub songs: "Ilkley Moor" and "Nellie Dean" and the rest. Everyone is friendly. It's a warm, cheerful evening. Then we are battling our way back along the Promenade towards the car.

Again Brenda sits between Brian and myself at the back. As the car moves off, Brenda settles into my arms and pulls my face down to hers. Rodney and Sylvia at the front are talking, not looking round. Enough light comes in from the streetlamps of Eastpool to show me Brian's face. It is grim, disapproving. I can understand his disapproval; can even, in a way, share it. I think of Ann as last I saw her, small and lost in the big, impersonal Imperial Hotel, saying wistfully that it's a long time till Tuesday. I love her. But I am kissing Brenda.

Stephen and Carolyn, if you have read as far as this you may well have a low opinion of the Philip Martin who is my former self. You cannot feel more harshly towards him than I have done as I write this account. The temptation to revise just a little, to omit just a little, to present a portrait without warts, has been enormous. But there would be no point in going to all this trouble if I were not to tell the

*truth, or as much of it as I can now recall. I love
Ann but I am kissing Brenda.*

In the front of the car, Rodney and Sylvia chatter happily. Now and again Sylvia's clear laugh rings out. Sylvia
—healthy, well-balanced, resilient, naturally high-spirited
—will not break her heart; has not broken her heart. She
will come through this episode unscathed.

Mr. Fox has a radio in his car, and Rodney switches it
on for the news. We hear the time signal, the sober BBC
voice. A few preliminary words. Then, "It is announced
tonight that a nonaggression pact has been signed between Germany and the Soviet Union."

The car swerves and recovers.

"God!" says Rodney. "My God!"

"What does it mean, Rodney?" Sylvia asks.

"It means the green light for Hitler to invade Poland.
And you know what *that* means?"

"I suppose so."

"It means that war isn't a probability any more. It's a
certainty. And it won't be long . . . Oh, well, I'm glad we
had today, anyway. It was a good day, wasn't it?"

"It was a very good day," Sylvia says. "Thank you, Rodney."

I detach myself from Brenda.

"Rodney," I ask, "will you go?"

"I expect so."

"As a volunteer?"

"I might."

"But I thought you were against war."

"There are times," says Rodney, "when you may not want
to be playing, but if the ball comes your way you can't
just let it pass."

"It's not much of a game."

"Maybe not, but it'd be nasty if the other lot won."

"Good old Rodney," says Brenda—whether ironically or seriously I shall never know.

"Poor old world," says Rodney.

22

Tuesday the twenty-second. My father is up in good time, waiting impatiently for the newspaper. When it arrives he spreads it out on the breakfast table, standing up to study it. The radio bulletin is confirmed, of course. Huge headlines about the Nazi-Soviet Pact.

"Well, this looks like it," Father says. "I don't know what to say. It's horrible to think of another war. But—" he hesitates for a long time, then says it—"it'll save the firm."

"War work?" my mother asks.

"War work. There'll be plenty for us, while ever it lasts. Service clothing, uniforms . . . So long as we get our contracts properly drawn up, we can't go wrong."

"It's an ill wind, I suppose," Mother says heavily, "that blows nobody any good."

There is more shame than satisfaction in the air. I see now why my casual remark at the start of the holiday was so hurtful to Father.

"You *did* keep the factory going for this, didn't you?" I

ask. My tone of voice is not aggressive, and Father doesn't take offense.

"We'd have closed a year ago," he says, "if I hadn't thought it was coming." And then, "Don't be too shocked, Phil. By hanging on, I've saved a hundred people's jobs. And what would I have done if I'd fallen out of work last year at my age? Where would we have been? And the Pillings?"

"We'd have sold these bungalows, I expect," says Paula practically.

"And we wouldn't have been at Linley this August," I say, "and I'd never have . . ." But I let my voice trail away.

"Anyway," Father says with an obvious effort to be brisk and matter-of-fact, "I've no business to be away from the office now. A lot depends on how we handle things in the next few days. Too much cut-throat competition in this trade to let us take things easy. I must get back right away."

"When are you going, dear?" Mother asks.

"Soon as we're ready."

" 'We'? We can't all pack up and go at a moment's notice."

"No need to close the bungalow," Father says. "If all goes well we'll be able to come back and clear up at leisure. We might even stay for a few more days. But I *must* get back to the office this morning."

"You could look after yourself, perhaps," Mother suggests to him tentatively.

"I'll be busy, dear. I won't have time to order milk and cook meals."

"You could stay at the King's Hotel."

Father goes across to Mother, puts his hands on her shoulders, looks into her eyes appealingly.

"You know what I think about staying at the King's," he says. "You know who I like to have with me."

Mother doesn't even sigh.

"All right," she says.

"Anyway," Father goes on, "don't forget you're the principal shareholder. At a time like this I oughtn't to act without the principal shareholder's approval."

"At other times you manage," Mother says. But seeing that Father is beginning to look hurt she smiles and says, "Of course I'll come. And that means Alison must come, too. What about Paula and Philip?"

"Oh, yes, Philip," my father says. "That reminds me. We have to face facts, Phil, and the fact is that I'd better get you into the firm as soon as possible. With any luck we'll be able to prove you're on vital war work by the time your call-up comes."

I stare. I have never been a rebel, have never had any distaste for the family business. I've always supposed I shall go into it eventually, if it's still there. But Father's remark comes as a shock. What he proposes, though well meant so far as I am concerned, sounds altogether too neat and smacks too much of privilege. And why have I spent three years in the school training corps if I'm going to be kept out of the Army?

But before I can say anything Father goes on, "We'll talk about that later. No time now. I don't want you in the office this week, Phil, you wouldn't know what it was all about and you'd only be in the way. Stay here if you like."

"I think we'd both rather stay," says Paula. "And we could look after Alison."

But Alison wants to go home.

"It's raining again," she complains, "and there's nobody here of my age to play with, and if I go home there'll be Sally-next-door, and I'll like it much better."

[190]

"Well, there we are," says Mother. "It looks as if everything's decided. I'll just pack the essentials. We can be ready in half an hour."

"Twenty minutes would be an improvement," says Father.

Then there's a tap on the door and Rodney comes in.

"Hello, Rodney," Father says. "You were right all the time, weren't you? I owe you half a crown."

"Not just yet," says Rodney. "But you soon will, I'm afraid. Pay up when war's declared." He turns to me and Paula.

"How about coming down to our place? Syl and Brian are there. We're going to try the new board game we brought with us. It's terrifically complicated. You spend half a day studying the rules and the rest of the week playing the game. But in weather like this, with nothing to do but wait for the news, what else can we do but a bit of fiddling while Rome burns?"

"You're keeping us all organized these days, aren't you, Rodney?" I remark. "I can't believe it."

"Rodney rallies round again," says Rodney. And Paula gets the next three words in ahead of him:

"Good old Rodney."

The board game involves complicated financial maneuverings with vast sums of imaginary money. It doesn't actually take half a day to learn the rules, but it does take the best part of an hour, and it soon looks as though the first game could last well into the afternoon. Rodney, the unbeliever who enjoys singing hymns, is also a Socialist with an apparent talent for capitalism. He does well and looks set to win. Except for Brenda and myself, the others are pretty competent, too.

By midday I've had enough, and I have a growing awareness that I ought to be somewhere else. I find that although it takes a long time to win this game, the road to ruin can be short. Soon after lunch I make some deliberately disastrous investments, and am bankrupt and out of the game. I excuse myself and leave.

Brenda goes with me to the gate. She is serving a prison sentence for fraud and has to miss three turns.

"You're going to see *her,* aren't you? Miss Skinny?"

"Her name is Ann."

"You were only playing about last night with me, only fooling, I know. You don't care tuppence for me, do you?"

I don't say anything to that.

"I wonder how she'd have liked it, if she'd seen. Anyway, I bet you don't have much fun with *her.* . . . Do you think you're clever, Phil?"

"No. Far from it."

"Do you think you're *nice?*"

"As a matter of fact, no."

"Well, I agree with you there. You're not. I don't know why I like you."

"You don't have to like me."

"I don't like you because I *want* to," Brenda says. "I wish I didn't. I think boys are awful. I don't know why they were invented."

"I expect you'll find out," I say drily.

This makes her giggle.

"I expect I will," she says. "It doesn't look as if I'll learn it from you, though."

But there's no malice in Brenda.

"Oh, well, if that's the way things are, I might as well go back and see if I'm due to come out of jail."

"That's the spirit. I hope you throw lots of sixes."

"Actually," says Brenda, "I think games are an awful bore, don't you? I'd never play games if there was anything better to do."

Ann said it was a long time till Tuesday. Now it's Tuesday. It's been Tuesday for hours. A wet and windy Tuesday. I stand in Middle Row. I haven't hurried to get here. And now I'm here I'm hesitating.

I want to see Ann desperately. I think she wants to see me desperately. At the same time I don't want to see her. It's an agony of longing and reluctance. It doesn't make sense, and I ought to stop and sort it out methodically, but I can't bring myself to do that. There are too many facts I don't want to face.

I wonder if she's here in the Partingtons' cottage. Probably she is. Her mother will be away on her day off. Ann said she'd be here, and there's no reason why she shouldn't be; she doesn't like staying in the hotel. I can't see any sign of occupation from the street; but then, there never *is* any sign of occupation. We are careful about that.

I stand, still hesitating. I am really looking at the cottages for the first time in three weeks. Usually I just come down here and try to get inside as quickly as possible without being seen. Now I feel a slight panic on Ann's behalf; she keeps coming here and it isn't really safe. But the feeling goes. The cottages don't look any different. Maybe they'll last for weeks, months, a year. I'm beginning to think they'll never go at all.

Now the sky is clearing. The wind has dropped a little and is steadier. And the urge comes on me once more to be away from land, to be out on my own. Without having sorted anything out, I turn and walk on towards the slipway.

Somehow I hadn't expected to find Harold here. But here he is. He's sitting on the upturned boat, as so often before, but today he's not baiting lines. He is reading the newspaper. The ugly headlines are towards me. Harold is reading the sports page at the back. He looks up and says, "You're not wanting *Seasprite* today, are you?"

"As a matter of fact I am. Can I have her?"

"For crying out loud. She's not rigged. It isn't worth it. You're a nuisance, Phil. . . . Oh, all right, you can have her, if you'll give me a hand."

Harold and I rig the boat together.

"You're on your way tomorrow, aren't you?" I ask.

"Aye. I thought you'd have known that well enough, after the trouble the other night."

He grins.

"She was fierce, wasn't she? And that brother of hers. I thought they'd have murdered me, between them."

"Sylvia wasn't very pleased that you'd arranged to go and visit a pal in your last few days," I point out. "And that you hadn't bothered to tell her. You can't blame her, really, Harold, if she took it as a bit of an insult. She felt it showed you didn't care about her. Wouldn't you have felt the same if it had been the other way round?"

Harold considers the matter.

"I reckon not," he says after a little thought. And then, "Well, you know how it is, Phil. Lasses are all very well, but the time comes when you want to be with a pal. Somebody you can have a couple of beers with, and swap a joke or two, and talk football. Whereas with lasses, you feel they're always hanging round your neck, wondering if you like their new dress and wanting to know if you really love them. You get to feel you've had enough of it."

"Sylvia's not like that, Harold. She wouldn't cling. She has her pride, and plenty of it."

"Oh, aye," says Harold. His tone is conciliatory. "Don't get me wrong, Phil. I've nothing against Sylvia. Nice girl. One of the best. But, well—the fact is, when you've only a few days left you have to make the most of them, haven't you? Old Len's my best pal, and I haven't seen him for a year. I mean, there's plenty of lasses around, but real pals are scarce. You don't want to lose them, do you?"

I look at Harold's face, trying to see him through fresh rather than familiar eyes. He is blond enough, handsome enough, to attract the girls wherever he goes. Perhaps you can't blame him for thinking there's an endless supply and one is much the same as another. And yet I'm annoyed on behalf of girls in general and Sylvia in particular.

"Sylvia's not just one of plenty," I tell him. "Sylvia's special. I feel about her the way you might feel about a pal."

"No offense meant," says Harold. "Tell her I'm sorry. Tell her I'll miss her. Tell her anything you like if it'll make her happy. And now, watch that mainsheet, Phil, it's getting all in a tangle. Here, what about paying me? How long you planning to be out?"

"I don't know. Haven't thought about it. It depends on the weather."

"It doesn't matter, then. Pay when you come in. If it isn't me, it'll be my grandpa."

"What's the weather going to be like, anyway?"

"Oh, all right. Sea won't get any rougher, I reckon. Might rain again, though. Like I said before, when it comes to sailing, I'd sooner it be you than me. O.K., Phil, off you go."

I sail *Seasprite* out, quite a long way out to sea. The sky is clear for the moment. There's not another sail on the bay. But the usual therapy of wind and water doesn't quite work. I find I'm thinking of navies, blockades, convoys, sinkings. And the sea, after all, is not a friendly element—not what we were designed for.

I sail back in towards Linley. Then I tack two or three

times, aimlessly in and out. And then, without conscious intention, I find I'm heading for the tiny cove with the old jetty, where we were before. I tie *Seasprite* up and sit on the sand. This must be just about where Ann and I built our sand castle. And over there was where Harold fell asleep.

I sit with my back against a rock and think. There's so much to think about that it all jostles around in my mind, trying to push its way to the front. About the war, mainly, and how it's going to affect us all. My father talks about saving the firm, but I wonder whether there'll be any firm to save, or anybody to save it *for*. I recall the films and novels about gas warfare. Maybe Hitler's secret weapon will be a new poison gas, and within a few weeks we'll all be choking or blistering to death. . . .

But at last my thoughts find their way where they had to go in the end: to Ann. I must throw the garbage out of my mind and think, think clearly, whatever it costs.

All right, then: about Ann. I love her. Meaning what? It'd be easy if I were Romeo and she were Juliet and love was a simple elemental force, never to be denied this side of the grave. It'd be just as easy if it were all a matter of glands and instincts, and fidgety bits of the body wanting to be eased. But people—muddled, complicated people in a muddled, complicated world—make things difficult, too difficult by half.

I must face it. There's a part of me that simply wants to sail away from Ann; there always has been. I don't want to get involved. There's no point in getting involved. She won't be here next year, neither will I. It's just a holiday encounter. As Harold says, there's plenty of lasses around; and a good many of them are more exciting than Ann Tarrant.

And most of the millions of others haven't been in a

sanatorium. I must face this, too. I share the fear the word arouses in people's minds. My mother's remarks have made it stronger. Mother is not a silly, not a vindictive person. She's merely cautious on behalf of her child; me. Love conquers all things, they say, but does it conquer this?

Mother thought it would be kinder to Ann not to get involved. I have told Sylvia that Ann would be well rid of me. Maybe this is true. Maybe I've been helping her build up an illusion, and the further it's built up the more she'll be hurt when it shatters. Do I believe this, or is it a smoke screen to cover my own withdrawal? I don't know. But it would be so easy to up-anchor and go. If I wanted to be really courteous I could write Ann a little note saying I was sorry I hadn't managed to see her again. And put it in the post. The splendid, impersonal, insulating post.

Then there's the resentment I feel against Ann. Silly resentment, for not being what she isn't, for not understanding things she couldn't understand. But hell, I'm only human. I have spent a night with her in the Partingtons' cottage, and gone away frustrated in the morning. It's more fun to cuddle with Brenda in the back of a car than to engage in quaint little sir-and-madam conversations with Ann.

And yet after all I love her, I'm committed. Not as a charity; I have no more to give her than she to give me. The world is full of lasses; yes; but it's Ann alone who has come clear and unique for me, her individual self. In a way nothing has happened between us; in another way a good deal has happened. A relationship that wasn't meant to be brief, that ought to have taken years, has tried desperately to root itself and flower. Planted in poor thin soil for a short season, it's lived, and it's living still. Like one of those scrawny plants in a pot in the back yard. I can't just throw it in the bin; or can I? It will never be beautiful, rich, fully-developed; fit to win a prize in a garden show. But a flower, however humble, is a flower.

Even now, I don't know where I am. I said I'd see her on Tuesday. It's still Tuesday. It will be Tuesday for a few hours yet.

The sky is clouding again. To get back to Linley I must beat to windward, but the wind is still dropping. It's a slow, laborious business. I'd get there more quickly if I lowered the sail and rowed. But I won't do that; it's ignominious. And I am not in a hurry.

It's early evening when I come to the slipway. Old Mr. Ericson is there. He's had plenty of time to notice my approach, and he's waiting for me with the trolley.

"I nearly left you to it, lad," he says. "But I didn't want you to rupture yourself."

"How much do I owe you?"

"Nothing today. You can buy me a drink if you like. Just help me put the boat away and come over to the Fo'c'sle. It's Harold's farewell."

The Fo'c'sle is poky, low-ceilinged, but comfortable. There's a fire, and it's needed, for the night is not warm. Everyone is drinking ale.

"How old are you, lad?" asks Tom Thorp, the landlord, before serving me; but his expression invites me to lie, and I do. Harold greets me like a favorite brother. He won't let me buy Mr. Ericson a drink; he is treating everybody. Harold and I in fact are the only two young people in the place. There are two or three middle-aged men, but the rest are the local old codgers. Bergs and Billingtons, Thorps and Olsens; men with long memories of the sea.

There's much naval reminiscence, for most of them seem to have been in the Navy at one time or another. They tell stories of the Great War; rambling tales that I guess to have been told two, three, or ten times already.

Halfway through the evening, Mr. Fox comes in. It surprises me to see him in the Fo'c'sle; I thought the Imperial Bar was more his style; but they know and greet him. A battle develops between Mr. Fox and Harold over the buying of drinks. Mr. Fox pumps Harold's hand repeatedly, and tells him he's joining a great service and the country will be grateful for lads like him.

Then for a while Mr. Fox sits beside me. He tells me with pride about the accuracy of Rodney's forecasts.

"He knew all along it was coming," he says. "The rest of us were taken in, but not Rodney. He has a brain, you know, he has a brain. Mark my words, young Rodney'll go far."

"Let's hope it's over soon," says old Mr. Ericson.

"Over by Christmas *this* time," Mr. Fox predicts. "Hitler's not the Kaiser, he's only a jumped-up corporal. Two or three defeats and he'll be out on his ear. Then they'll sue for peace."

"Is that what Rodney says?" I ask.

"No," admits Mr. Fox. For a moment he's downcast. Then he cheers up and says, "Even our Rodney doesn't know everything. It'll do him good to find he's not always right. Who'll have another pint?"

Towards closing time, Mr. Fox insists on buying whiskies all round. Then he has us joining hands and singing "Auld Lang Syne" in Harold's honor. Afterwards, in the street, there are prolonged leavetakings and expressions of esteem all round. The old chaps trudge or hobble towards their homes. Most have drunk several pints of ale, but it doesn't seem to have affected them.

Harold explains loudly to all who will listen that he's normally cold sober from one year's end to the next, but that he meant to get drunk tonight and he's done it. He goes off happily, leaning on his grandfather.

"I'll give you a lift, Phil," says Mr. Fox. It's more a command than an offer. And the part of me that's been precariously in charge for much of the day, the part that wants to slink away without seeing Ann, would be glad to obey and get safely back to the family bungalow. But as night draws on the more positive parts are taking control, beginning to jostle each other for position, refusing to be thrust aside.

"Thank you," I say to Mr. Fox, "but I think I ought to help see Harold home."

"That's right," says Mr. Fox approvingly. "Never desert a pal. And, Phil, you may be proud some day to have known Harold Ericson. Proud to tell folk you helped put him to bed the night before he left to join the Navy."

Harold consents to give me his other arm and walk between Mr. Ericson and myself. But he's not so drunk as he chooses to seem. Having put on a good public performance, so that all those present will be able to tell in colorful detail the story of his last night at Linley, he recovers smartly as soon as there is nobody in sight.

"Coming in, lad?" old Mr. Ericson asks. Harold says, "Nay, let him get on his way," but I accept the offer and sit in the Ericsons' kitchen. Harold's grandfather brings out bread and cheese and pickles, and I'm glad of the food because I haven't eaten since lunch. Harold takes off his boots, and half-sits, half-lies on an ancient sofa. A surprisingly businesslike discussion takes place between the two of them on the future prospects of fishing, boat-hiring, and Mr. Ericson's retirement.

Mr. Ericson produces from a cupboard a bottle of Dutch gin. He winks.

"You know Linley Bottom was a great place for smuggling in the old days," he says. "Well, there's some who say the odd drop of liquor might still have found its way in, up to a year or two ago. I'm not passing any opinion on that. But you haven't seen *this* brand before, have you, lad?"

Normally I'd steer clear of Dutch gin, especially on top of beer and a double whisky. But tonight the thought is still high in my mind that war's about to start and I'll soon be old enough to fight; and if I'm old enough to fight I'm old enough to drink what I like. I accept a glass, and down it almost as quickly as Mr. Ericson. He refills it.

Harold and his grandfather continue the business discussion. Obviously both of them are a good deal clearer-headed than I am. I am confused and tired; the long active day is over and more than over. But the night has only begun, and to the night there are new responses; they are not tired.

Harold says, "Well, I'll be getting my head down. Have to make an early start in the morning." Obviously it's time for me to go. And I'm ready to go. I make my farewells briefly, since the formal occasion is over, and let myself out into the street.

I can walk steadily. Fairly steadily.

Raining again and dark; no moon and not much wind. In the night silence the sea is audible: breathing gently in its sleep, no malice in it.

Now is my last chance to slip away: up the main street to Top Square, then along Bay Road to the bungalows, and so to bed. Safer in every respect. But I'm no longer considering it.

Of course Ann could be back at the hotel, fast asleep. But she's not at the hotel; I know she isn't. Every instinct tells me that with her mother away she'll be spending this

[201]

night in the secret, the private place. Whether I am there or not.

I said I'd see her on Tuesday. There's half an hour of Tuesday left. I can still make it.

23

No moon, but it's never quite dark here, and the little row of cottages looms on the cliff edge. Suddenly the impulse comes upon me to get to the Partingtons' by the outside path—the way I took on my first visit, three weeks ago. I'm sober enough to see where I'm going, and far enough outside my usual self to feel a vast improvement in my head for heights. The whisper of the sea below is almost reassuring. I shan't slip, I shan't put a foot wrong; and if I did, I could float through the air.

I edge my way past the first cottage; the boarded door, the boarded window. Now round the downspout that spouts on to nothing. It's dead easy; I can't think why I was scared the previous time. I almost run past the second cottage. Then my foot slips on wet soil and I am sliding. I am reaching out, but there's nothing there. I am sliding, sliding.

It's the end. I made a mad decision and it's the end. My hand has grabbed the half-rooted tree that hangs over the slope. That's slowed me; halted me for the moment; but it's not strong enough. I can feel its remaining roots giving way under the strain; can hear them crack. It's not holding me any more. I'm on my face now, stomach pressed to the slope, feet farthest down. I scrabble, unable to find any further hand or foothold. Sliding again. Then, at the farthest reach of my left arm, a jutting bit of masonry, solid.

I'm holding it with one hand, then two. My feet still working; scratching and slipping. Nothing else in reach. I feel weak. Shock, drink, fatigue—I don't know what it is, but there's no strength in me.

If she's in the cottage, she's only a few feet away: to my left and above, for I've slid farther down than even the basement of the Partingtons'. I bellow, "Ann! Ann!"

No response, except a slight echo from a cliff face farther along towards North Bay. The sea still murmuring below, but not reassuring now; just indifferent. Rain, light but steady.

"Ann! Ann!"

It's a cliffhanger. The thought makes me want to laugh, absurdly. Yes, literally, it's a cliffhanger. I'm clinging to an outcrop of some cottage's foundations—perhaps the Partingtons', perhaps the last remnant of one that's gone already. Come along next week to the kids' matinee and see how our hero gets out of this one.

But what if he doesn't?

"Ann! Ann!"

Either she's not here or she's asleep and isn't going to hear me. This is all silly, unbelievable. I can't really be in danger of death. It just isn't a possibility. If she doesn't come or I get weaker I shall let go. It doesn't have to be the end. If I cling, if I don't let myself slide too fast, if the cliff doesn't get too suddenly steeper, I might not be hurt, or not much. There could even be some kind of resting place before the bottom.

"Ann! Ann!"

"Philip! Where on earth *are* you?"

She's there above me. I start laughing, helplessly, almost hysterically.

"Here I am! Here I—ha ha ha—am!"

I'm laughing, though I don't know what's funny about it. Neither does she.

"Where?" She shines a flashlight. "Oh, my goodness! You can't move, can you?"

"No." I am laughing again.

"Can you hold on a minute?"

That's funny too. Can I hold on a minute, as if it was the telephone? A good question, though. I'd better.

"Yes, I can hold on."

Then she's hanging on to something with one hand and holding something out to me with the other. Could be an old chair. It doesn't look promising, and surely she's not strong enough to take my weight. But she's giving me some kind of support as I scrabble again and grab; and without knowing just what's happened I am hauling myself up over the edge and on to the tiny paved area beside the basement.

I stand upright, stagger, half-fall, and send a dozen pot plants crashing to the paved surface. But I'm there; safe and more or less sound. I straighten up. Ann puts down the old chair and faces me. She's wearing a dressing gown.

"Philip!" Her voice is a bit husky. "Philip, what *is* going on? What have you been doing?"

The church clock begins to strike.

"I said I'd see you on Tuesday." I giggle, absurd lout

that I am. "I said I'd see you on Tuesday. I made it, just."

The clock finishes striking.

"Now it's Wednesday," I inform her.

"Come inside, Philip."

She leads the way upstairs from basement to kitchen, then up again into the Partingtons' main bedroom. The curtains are drawn and it's pitch black. Shining her flashlight, Ann picks out the little oil lamp.

"I'll light it," I say. I have some trouble in getting the match to the right spot, but at last the lamp flickers and burns up. Ann sits on the bed, almost sinking on to it.

"Ann! Are you all right?"

"I'm all right." Her voice still sounds husky; perhaps a bit shaky, too. But then, she's had a shock. So have I.

"You've been here all day?"

"Mmm."

"You must have thought I wasn't coming."

She nods.

"You were in bed?"

"Yes. I . . . brought my own sheets. I'm not using theirs."

"And it's your own dressing gown you're wearing?"

"Yes."

"You *were* prepared."

"I always meant to stay."

"Ann, you're shivering."

"It's nothing."

"You're *sure* you're all right?"

"Yes. I . . . You frightened me for a minute. Seeing you out there on the cliff face like that."

"You're still trembling."

"I do feel a bit shivery," she admits.

"Get back into bed, then."

She takes off the dressing gown. Clasping her white nightdress round her ankles, she edges herself into the bed. As she does so, another great shiver runs through her.

I move into the pool of light, and she says, "Philip! You've got mud all over you. Oh, Philip, what did you *mean* by coming round the outside like that? I *told* you it was dangerous. And to do it at night, and when it's all wet and slippery! It might have been the end of you."

This is where I ought to apologize, and tell her she's saved my life. But I don't feel like apologizing. My thoughts and feelings are all out of gear tonight. Seeing her sitting in bed in her white cotton nightdress, I find that my resentments of earlier in the day are making a shameful comeback. And they're accompanied by other sensations.

"What if it *had* been the end of me? What's it matter?"

"What's it matter?" she echoes. "My goodness, I should think it matters!"

"Don't you know there's a war just starting?" I demand.

"They were talking about it at the hotel. I didn't quite understand. It hasn't actually begun yet, has it?"

"Not that I know of. But it soon will."

She doesn't say anything. Her face is only a blur on the edge of the pool of lamplight.

"It's not like the Great War, you know," I go on. "Then everybody felt heroic. Till they found out what it was really like. Well, this time we aren't under any illusions. Nobody in his right mind expects to enjoy it . . . You know where I've been tonight?"

"No. How could I?"

"I've been at the Fo'c'sle, seeing Harold Ericson off to join the Navy."

"I did rather think . . ."

"You thought you smelled something, eh? Do I reek? Well, what does that matter, either?" I go on, my voice rising: "You know what? In two weeks' time I'll be seventeen. In a year and two weeks, if I haven't been bombed or gassed, I'll be eighteen. Old enough to get a bayonet through my guts."

I stand outside and hear myself saying this, and I know it is silly, stale, self-pitying, corny, but I am saying it just the same, and part of me is enjoying it.

"Don't, Philip!" She shudders again.

" 'Don't, Philip, don't!' " Now I am mimicking her. " 'Don't say anything unpleasant. Just play a nice quiet game of house.' My God, do you know what century you're living in? Do you know *anything?*"

My head is swimming. I'm sure I'm not drunk. It's quite a while now since that last glass of Dutch gin at the Ericsons'. The effect must be wearing off. But there seems to be a lot of liquid swirling around inside me. And a night like this is not normal life. There's never been a night like it; there'll never be another night like it. I don't feel responsible for what I do; still less for what I say.

"A good job for you that you haven't tried this game with Harold Ericson," I tell her. *"He* wouldn't be a nice, well-behaved ninny like me, I can tell you!"

"Philip, you're not a ninny."

"I'm *some* kind of fool, I know that!"

Here she is, in her nightdress, in bed, and here am I, just standing and looking at her.

But my head is spinning more. And the level of liquid seems perilously high inside me. I don't feel ill, but I feel unstable.

"It's always the same," I complain. "I'm grown up for *some* purposes. Other people's purposes. Not my own."

My God, I'm unstable. Dangerously unstable. And the instability is mounting to my throat. Suddenly the position is desperate.

"Excuse me," I say in absurd anticlimax, and am hurrying from the room.

I don't go to the bathroom. There's no need for that when you're on a cliff edge with the sea below. And anyway, our primitive arrangements for flushing with a water jug couldn't cope with this. I go out to the paved area and lean over.

For a moment I think I can avoid it. But I'm full; full of everything; and everything has to come. It's worse than I thought.

A minute later I feel empty, unbelievably empty, almost turned inside out, but retching still. I stagger back at last, sink on to the bench where we sat together in the sun a few days ago. My forehead is cold and damp. And along with the swirl of liquid and the confusion in my head, my excitement has gone.

The rain, which had stopped, starts again, not heavy but fresh and welcome. I am better already. Not just physically better; I am thinking and feeling clearly again.

I am not thinking of a girl in bed, resenting her, wanting a male triumph. I am thinking that this is Ann, and she is vulnerable, and I love her dearly. And I am feeling anxious for her; because surely she is not well and shouldn't be shivering like that.

I go back inside.

"Philip, are you all right?" she asks. Her voice is low but alarmed.

"I'm all right. Are *you* all right?" Now I go towards her and put my face, still white-feeling, still with a chilly sweat on the forehead, down to hers.

"I shouldn't come too close, Philip," she says.

"Ann! What is it?"

"It's nothing. Just a cold that began on Sunday. It was a bit feverish at first, but it's better now. By tomorrow I'll be fine."

"But oughtn't you—?"

"Oughtn't I what? To be in bed? I *am* in bed."

"To see a doctor, I mean."

"At this time of night? Oh, Philip, do believe me, it's nothing. If I'd needed to see the doctor, I'd have gone before."

"If you're not better, you must go first thing in the morning."

"Yes, sir," she says. In the poor light I can see the glimmer of a smile.

"Oh, Ann, why didn't you *tell* me? Instead of letting me carry on like that?"

"It didn't seem important. Such a little thing, compared with what was worrying *you*."

"It was more important."

"Philip, you've still got mud all over you. Put your things down carefully in the bathroom, and we'll see if we can brush the mud off in the morning."

"If you're better."

"I shall be better. Philip, there's a pair of Mr. Partington's pajamas in that drawer. You could borrow them. I don't suppose he'd mind, in the circumstances."

"He'd have other things to mind about if he turned up tonight."

"Goodness, he'd better *not* turn up!"

"Can I really—join you, after what I said?"

"I want you to. But I don't want you to catch my cold."

"Oh, that."

Mr. Partington's pajamas are canary-yellow flannelette, and far too big for me. Even in the lamplight the effect is absurd. We both laugh. Ann's laugh turns into a slight cough.

I climb into bed, still laughing.

"Thank you, Mr. Partington," I say. "You can borrow *my* pajamas, if ever you need to."

"I'm afraid they wouldn't do for him," Ann says. "I shouldn't think they'd go halfway round." We giggle again. Then, "Philip, this isn't a game. It's . . . all right."

But the excitement left me when I was outside and won't be back for a while. And if it comes back I can cope with it. I know that for Ann it isn't time, and I don't feel resentful any more. I love her.

I hold her, and she is still chilly and gives another shiver, but then she begins to thaw into me.

"You really ought to turn your face away," she says.

"I'm not going to. Breathe into my mouth, breathe all over me, I don't mind."

"Whatever I have, you'll share it?" she asks.

"Yes."

"I haven't anything you wouldn't want, Philip. Except this cold. I haven't, truly. You believe me, don't you?"

"Of course."

"I hope you do. If there was any doubt I wouldn't let you be so close . . . We are close, aren't we?"

"Hardly separate at all."

We lie awake for quite a long time, not saying much. At first we can hear the sea, talking to itself beneath us; later its sound is lost in that of the rain, which grows heavier, beating on roof and windowpane. We leave the lamp on so that we can see each other's faces, but we turn it low, because there isn't much oil in it.

We've been silent for a while when Ann says, "You snored."

"I didn't. I never snore."

"You did. Just a little one. It was quite a *nice* snore, Philip . . . Perhaps I'd better put the light out."

"I don't specially want to, do you?"

"No, I don't want it to be the end of the day. Or do I mean the end of the night? I don't know what I mean, Philip. Everything's so *strange*. But I feel content. Almost as if my life had been completed."

"Completed? What a funny thing to say. It's hardly begun."

"Well, we don't know what will happen, do we? Specially at present. We have to be thankful for what we've had already."

"Don't turn the lamp off, Ann. Let it burn itself out."

I can still see her face, and she's happy. In the near-darkness the happiness flows between us: from her to me and back, strengthened, into her. If she's happy I'm happy; it's the deepest happiness I know.

24

It seems to me afterwards that we had our warning; that during the night we both heard a cracking sound, felt a deep tremor. But it seems it must have come when our sleep was deepest. It seems that we hardly surfaced to consciousness; that we drifted back to the safety of each other's arms.

It's lucky that only a bit of the cottage goes down.

In the morning it goes, at just after seven o'clock. A shudder, a rumble, a series of creakings and tearings. Not like the end of the world, but it shakes us awake. We jerk upright and see the end wall falling away, quite slowly, at leisure. There's dust and plaster in the air, a loose brick or two, but mostly the wall tilts back in one piece, like part of a building set, with window and frame still embedded in it.

And it's as though somebody had drawn back a great curtain, for the morning sun pours in from a clear blue sky. Through a light haze of dust we look into nothing; nothing but sea between us and the curved horizon.

The floor's not level now. A linen chest on castors moves slowly to the brink, tips partly over, and sticks. We jump out of bed, pull on clothes anyhow, hurry down a staircase that leans out of true. We're relieved to find we can still get through the connecting cupboards, over the archway, out into Lower Row. Alive, unhurt.

Across the way is the cottage with the pretty garden where, a few days ago, we saw the line of colorful washing. The door opens and the housewife comes out in her dressing gown. I know her. It's a Mrs. Olsen, one of three or four Mrs. Olsens in the village.

"Something gone over the edge, eh?" she says.

"I reckon so," I answer cautiously. I look sideways at Ann. She is pale, a little shaken, but seems no worse than last night.

"Looks like it's the far end of the Partingtons'," Mrs. Olsen says. She studies, appraisingly, the rest of the little row of cottages on their frail peninsula.

"Will they all go, do you think?" I ask her.

"Can't say. It's the heavy rain that's done it; no help from the sea. It may be just a little slide. If the rest of them last another ten minutes, they could hang on for weeks."

We wait. I hold Ann's hand. Nothing more happens. After a while Mrs. Olsen leads us to a point, a little farther along the cliff, from which we can see what's happened. And really it's nothing much; it doesn't look dramatic at all. There isn't even a clean new edge to the cliff. There's just a small, unimpressive heap of soil and masonry and rubble, lying there for the sea to suck at and digest at leisure. From it rises a little dust, like the last smoke of a dying fire.

"I wondered once or twice if there was a young couple

going in and out of there," says Mrs. Olsen. She eyes us suspiciously. "Looked a bit like you," she adds. "I nearly went and told them, 'It's none of my business what you're up to, but you want to watch out.' Anyway, it doesn't look as if anyone got hurt. I hope that pair will have the sense to keep clear now."

"I'm sure they will."

"Of course, I may have been only imagining them," Mrs. Olsen goes on. "As I say, it's not my business. Oh, well, that's one step nearer my own house. It may be a few years yet, but our turn will come."

"It's awful," says Ann, "to think of your lovely garden being lost."

"It's life," says Mrs. Olsen. She goes back to her own door and closes it behind her.

"Ann," I say, "I want to get you straight back to the hotel. How are you, anyway?"

"I'm much better. I told you I would be. I feel a bit weak at the knees, but that's probably shock."

"Could be. I feel it too. Anyway, let's go."

Nobody else seems to have noticed yet that a little more cliff has gone. Ann and I walk up to the Imperial Hotel. It's a little before eight when we arrive.

Ann takes me down to the staff room. Somewhere she finds a brush, and we get most of the dried mud off my clothes. She seems to have recovered pretty well by now.

"I'm hungry," she says. "I didn't eat, yesterday. I didn't want a thing. But now I feel ready to make up for it." She fetches a plate of bacon and egg for each of us from the kitchen.

"Compliments of the chef," she says. "I told him I had a visitor, and he said he reckoned they owed me a meal or two. So here you are."

Everyone who's around this morning seems to know

and greet Ann, and it's all very friendly. She goes back for toast and marmalade. We munch and gossip. Nobody mentions war.

"Mother will be on the early train from Eastpool," Ann says at length. "I'd like to go and meet her." And we set off in the sunshine for the tiny station, adjoining Top Square. Perhaps it's a kind of nervous elation, and a reaction will set in later, but Ann is in high spirits and sings. She can't sing like Sylvia. She's not a patch on Sylvia, and I know we'll have to part before long, but I love her.

Halfway along the cliff path towards the North Bay bungalows, we stop and face each other.

"Sir," she says, "I fear our domestic establishment is no more."

" 'Fraid not," I answer in an ordinary tone. "Good-bye to the old home, in fact."

But she is playing our game once more.

"I am indebted to you, Mr. Martin," she says gravely, "for your kindness and consideration during the period of our acquaintance."

"An acquaintance which, if I may say so, has flowered into something deeper."

"Indeed, sir." She inclines her head in agreement.

And the thought comes into my mind: yes, it flowered. It flowered after all.

"Madam," I say, "the privilege and the pleasure have been mine."

She seems as if she's going to speak, then pauses. After a little while she says, "I'm tired of that game. I shall never play it again."

"Plain English now?" I ask.

"Yes. Plain English."

"All right. I love you, Ann."

"I love you, Philip. What will happen to us?"

"I don't know."

But I do know, and she knows, too.

We haven't even noticed Paula's approach, but she's standing a few feet away, waiting for us to take our eyes off each other.

"Father's back," she tells me when at last I look towards her.

"Back *already?* When did he arrive?"

"Half an hour ago. He drove through the night. I told him you'd gone out for an early walk."

"But what about Mother and Alison?"

"They're not with him. He's come to collect us, and all the stuff we can't leave at Linley. He says Parliament's been recalled and Britain's standing behind Poland and there's nothing left now but formalities before the shooting starts. And he wants us all to get home and prepare to dig in. It's going to last a long time."

Then she looks at Ann.

"I'm sorry, Ann," she says. "Especially about the other day. I hope I didn't spoil things for you."

Ann says thoughtfully, "No, nothing was spoiled."

To my surprise Paula kisses her.

Ann says, "Look, the train's coming. I want to be at the station when Mother arrives."

The little train is indeed chuffing round the headland from the direction of Eastpool.

Ann is moving away already. I have a sudden conviction that I'll never see her again.

"Write to me, Philip," she says.

"Good-bye, Ann," Paula and I call.

There's a bit of distance between us now as she hurries towards the station. Her voice floats back to us: "Good morning."

"Well," says Paula. "To start with, let's make some breakfast. Or have you had some, Phil?"

"Yes, I have. But I could eat some more."

"And then," Paula says, "we'll pack our stuff and say good-bye to the gang. Good-bye for now, that is. We'll be seeing them before long, of course."

"I expect so," I agree. And if we don't get blown to bits I am quite sure we shall. For whatever Rodney may say, the ties among the three families are strongly established. They'll hold for a few years yet.

As for Ann, she hasn't even said good-bye. That must have been deliberate. She only said "Good morning." It was the right farewell, though. A good morning is what we all have to wait for now. We may have to wait a long time. But it comes. After the dark, it comes.

25

Stephen and Carolyn, if you have read as far as this you know all I can tell you about the events of that summer at Linley Bottom. There was conceal-ment at the time—far too much of it—but there has been none in my narrative. I have told everything that was within my knowledge. On what was outside my knowledge I have not cared to speculate.

Perhaps I should tie up the loose ends, beginning with the small ones. I did not catch Ann's cold. The Partingtons never came back; it was learned after-wards that they had both died abroad that summer, within a few days of each other. By the time the heirs were traced there was nothing at Linley for them to inherit, for the rest of the cottage and its neighbors went down the cliff in November. But the pretty garden in Lower Row is still there, as pretty as ever. It is perched on the edge now, and will be next to go, having long outlived its former owners.

Father and I had several arguments about my joining the family firm to avoid call-up. He gave way in
the end, more or less gracefully. I stayed another
year at school, had a year at university—my only one
—then went into the Army. Oddly enough, when
the war was over I felt quite ready to go into the
firm. Later Brian joined me, and later still my sister
Alison. As you know, they are both directors now,
and better at business than I have ever been: more
efficient, more aggressive. The firm has never looked
back since 1939, which was its turning point. It isn't
a gold mine, but it's a prosperous concern. Sometimes, I have to admit, I find it a bore.

The war was the turning point for Paula, too. Father withdrew his objections and let her go to teachers' training college. He guessed correctly that
women would be called up, but was sure that teachers wouldn't have to go. Paula has done extremely
well, becoming a headmistress and afterwards Principal of a teachers' college herself. She has never
married; has never, I think, had any wish to do so.
She is successful, amiable, and happy as she is.

Soon after war started, the Army took over Linley
Bottom and much of the adjoining coast. Behind
barbed-wire entanglements it was rumored that anti-
invasion exercises took place. Later there were other
military and naval uses for Linley, and the war had
been over for three years before the Army moved
out. Linley never went back to normal, for it was
ripe to develop in a new direction. Today it is spick
and span, with plenty of antique and souvenir shops
to attract the tourist. Top Square has been turned
into an enormous parking lot, and there is a fine new
public lavatory, designed by the County Architect

and tastefully decorated in pastel shades. The railway, of course, has closed. Even the name has changed. Linley Bottom is dead, but Smugglers' Cove lives on.

I wrote twice to Ann, giving her my address, but I never got any reply. It's possible that her mother intercepted our letters; she was well placed to do so. In any case, they cannot have stayed at the Imperial for long. It closed down early in the war to become an officers' mess, and the staff dispersed.

Years afterwards, when the war was over, I made contact unexpectedly through Mrs. Billington at the shop. She'd had a letter out of the blue from Ann's mother, who had remarried. Ann had worked in a bookshop, then in libraries, then had gone to Australia as a librarian and married there. I wrote to her and we exchanged a letter or two, not saying much. Hers were the sort of letters she could have written with a husband looking over her shoulder; any kind of husband. The correspondence dwindled to Christmas cards. Two came from "Ann and Bob," two from "Ann, Bob, and Carolyn." Then a year with no card and a note received in February from Bob to say that she'd died. Not from tuberculosis, for what she had told me was of course true, and she was free of that disease. No, it was a road accident, in which Bob himself was badly hurt.

Somehow it was not a surprise that Ann died young. I wonder occasionally if the three and a half weeks for which I knew her were as important in her life as in mine. I think they may have been, but I shall never know. It was because of those three and a half weeks that I kept in touch with Bob and helped with the education of their child. I wish you could remember your mother, Carolyn, but of course you cannot.

The Foxes have outshone us all. Mr. Fox made a lot of money, lost it, and made a lot more. He served a six-month sentence for tax offenses and another for defrauding his creditors, but came out none the worse. Now he is a rich, happy, wicked old man. He still sometimes gives Mrs. Fox cause to come out with the same old shocked protest: "Bernie, please!"

Rodney, who had always refused to join the school training corps, threw up his university career and joined the Royal Air Force. He won the Distinguished Flying Cross, was shot down twice, and will limp for the rest of his life. The day he was demobilized, he shoved his Wing Commander's uniform in the bottom of a cupboard and told everyone that his rank henceforth was that of Mister. Now, as you know, he is a Member of Parliament; and, unlike some Members of Parliament, still unpredictable. Brenda became a G.I. bride on a rather exalted level, and her husband is now a college president; your college president. I do not know myself how you two came to be at the college together. Certainly it had nothing to do with me. But perhaps it was not entirely coincidence. Rodney and Brenda are both great fixers.

Mrs. Pilling—Sylvia's and Brian's mother—was the only one of us all to be killed in the war. She died in one of the few sporadic air raids on our city: on her way home from a friend's house where she'd been playing bridge. My own parents, as of course you know, are still fairly active in their retirement. We have been staying with them at Smugglers' Cove during the weeks in which I have written this account. *Harold Ericson served twelve years altogether in the Navy before returning here to marry fat, jolly Dorothy Thorp and settle down. His eldest son, Harold Ericson the twentieth, is a strapping lad who has inherited the Viking good looks.*

I was speaking to Harold only the other day. I still have to prompt him before he will call me "Philip," and he always refers to Sylvia as "Mrs. Martin" or "your wife." I have never asked, and never shall ask, Sylvia anything about the depth of her feeling for Harold, all those years ago. I have shown her this narrative, of course; I wouldn't have sent it to you if she'd disapproved; but she merely smiled, Sylvia-like, and said nothing. Sylvia has never had any difficulty in accepting people as they are, and this acceptance extends to the girl she used to be. I have found it harder. It has taken me a long time to come to terms with the young Philip Martin. There have been times in writing this account when I have disliked him intensely. But one must forgive everyone in the end, even oneself.

Stephen and Carolyn, you understand now why I wanted to tell you the story. It was not really so very great a coincidence that our son and Ann's daughter should come together, but when we first heard from you it was hard to believe. Since then we have come to see it as the happiest of occurrences. Maybe, in that strange year of 1939, we all got things wrong. You, I am sure, will get them right. That is what new generations are for.

> Sincerely,
>
> Philip